CW01080381

THE MULE'S FOAL

Fotini Epanomitis was born in Perth, Western Australia in 1969, the year her family migrated to Australia from Salonika in northern Greece. She spent most of her early life in Perth, except for a year living on her grandparents' farm in Greece when she was twelve. She has a Master of Arts degree in Literature from Curtin University in Western Australia and has taught literature at various universities throughout Australia. She has published short stories, articles and book reviews in a wide range of newspapers, journals and anthologies. Her first novel, *The Mule's Foal*, won the *Australian*/Vogel Literary Award, the Victorian Premier's Prize and was a regional winner of the Commonwealth Writers' Prize. Allen & Unwin will be publishing her second novel, *Fish Heads*, in 1998.

THE MULE'S FOAL

FOTINI EPANOMITIS

ALLEN & UNWIN

Publication of this title was assisted by the Australia Council, the Federal Government's arts funding and advisory body.

Australia Council for the Arts

First published in 1993
Reprinted 1993, 1994
This impression, 1997 by
Allen & Unwin
9 Atchison Street,
St Leonards, NSW 2065 Australia

First published in the U.K. in 1997 by
Allen & Unwin Ltd
London

National Library of Australia
Cataloguing-in-Publication entry:

Epanomitis, Fotini, 1969– .
The mule's foal.

ISBN 1 86373 454 6.

I. Title.

A823.3

Set in 10/15 pt Palatino by DOCUPRO, Sydney
Printed by Australian Print Group, Maryborough, Victoria

10 9 8 7 6 5 4

For my family

I would like to especially thank Professor Brian Dibble for his invaluable editorial advice and general guidance. I would also like to thank Rae Kelly and Helen Mumme for their assistance and patience when printing out the various drafts of this book.

Words borrowed from family and friends I return with many thanks.

ONE

IT'S BEEN A WHILE SINCE YOUNG FEET HAVE WALKED THE COBBLED STREETS OF THIS VILLAGE

It's been a while since young feet have walked the cobbled streets of this village. The young have moved to surrounding towns. What is there here for them? The valley dried up years ago, and anything you plant on the fields of the marshland just rots. Only old people live here. Greeks and Turks side by side, and they grow a little tobacco, just enough to chew on through the winter. When the sun falls, an insignificant and weary man wanders into the village, sings a song, and then he wanders out again.

At about this time of day you can see the shrivelled old woman in her black sack, crossing the bridge on her way to the outskirts of the village where there is a spring of water amidst some rocks. The story says that this is St. Vaia's holy water. St. Vaia, who had refused to abandon her faith for the Turks. They cut off her breasts and she bled to death. That is where the holy water is supposed to come from.

But then no one here remembers that story. The shrivelled

3

old woman who washes her body, taking special care never to unveil her face, is refreshed, if only temporarily. Now the people here do not remember the details. They live only on the general mood of things. And what a sad mood it is indeed. But no one knows exactly why. This is the village of amnesiacs, whereas once it was the village of gossips. If Meriklis the Grave-digger farted up one end of the village, by the end of that very same day every man, woman and child in the village would know about it. Mundane? Perhaps. But it was out of such mundane events that a rather extraordinary child came, bringing with it, for a while, such life, vivid and rich, as the village had never seen before.

If you come through this village, do not try to ask the shrivelled old woman why she crosses that bridge or why she veils her face. Do not try to ask the weary man what he is singing about. They do not know. I will tell you their story and you must take my word for it. Who else do you have? Agape rarely speaks. She just sits outside with pieces of wood and carves her ghastly figures. And Meta has never cared for stories.

This is the story of houses, of what happens in them and between them. This is the story of three houses. There is the House of Stefanos. Stefanos who was for a time the husband of Meta and the father of the feckless son, Theodosios. This is a house laid waste from the start.

Then there is the House of pappous Yiorgos. Pappous Yiorgos is the husband of yiayia Stella and the father of Vaia. This is an old house. A house that belongs to the daughters and the mothers of yiayia Stella. This is really the House of the Vaias. This house is mysterious.

Then there is our house. The house I have made with Meta and Agape of the Glowing Face. People have called our house a house of sin, but you can judge for yourself.

THE SHRIVELLED OLD WOMAN WHO VEILS HER FACE WAS ONCE A YOUNG GIRL The shrivelled old woman who veils her face was once a young girl, not a particularly beautiful one. In fact she was rather ugly. And there was nothing even extraordinary about her ugliness. In this village most people were ugly, and no one particularly cared. But there was something else. Vaia (as the girl was called) had a longing which kept her awake at nights. It was not a longing for ordinary things like love or money. It was a longing that no one talked about. But all the villagers saw it on her face. They said it was shameful for an unmarried girl to walk around with a face like that. So Pourthitsa the Matchmaker was commissioned. But as she pointed out, finding a match for this girl would be no easy task. How do you marry a girl with a face like that? Finally a rather ugly young man called Theodosios was found. No one else wanted to marry this ugly young man on account of a dark secret about his mother (a secret 6 which every man, woman and child in the village knew, and which will later be revealed to you). But, for the moment, it is enough to know that Theodosios and his seven brothers and sisters were brought up by their father alone. His name was Stefanos. His children were wild and unruly. In fact when his youngest daughter fell pregnant, it was said that her eldest brother was responsible. But the more sensible people of the village agreed that this was highly unlikely, and in any case children brought up without the love and guidance of a mother had to be judged under different laws.

So the marriage of Vaia and Theodosios was contracted and the villagers, satisfied with the whole affair, congratulated themselves. But the longing in Vaia's face did not go away. And, if they found this longing offensive in the unmarried girl's face, it was even more so in the married woman's. But then the marriage itself was certainly no ordinary marriage. It was not that the couple hated each other, but rather that they began their married life totally indifferent to each other. The villagers did not necessarily see this as a problem for, as yiayia Stella pointed out, most marriages were like this. However, what was particularly odd was that after the wedding night the groom never again spent a night in his wife's bed. When the sun went down, he would set off for his father's house and he would spend every night in his father's house.

7   The longing in Vaia's face grew worse and worse till

it became obscene. The girl could not leave the house, not even to work in the fields. She became totally consumed by the longing and broke out in a fever. Yiayia Stella, fearing her daughter would die, sent pappous Yiorgos to fetch the doctor. The doctor gave Vaia a medicine which made the fever go down and, after examining her, pronounced that she was pregnant. Now you can just imagine everyone's surprise at this news, but then all agreed that it was surely a good thing.

Vaia did get better and returned to the fields. Theodosios still spent his nights at his father's, but Vaia's longing seemed to disappear. And for the first time the couple began to disagree. They spent all day in the fields arguing.

In this village it was an old custom to name the children after the yiayies and the pappouthes. And one day in the fields Vaia mentioned to her husband that their child would be named after her father. Of all the things his wife could have said, nothing could have angered Theodosios as this did.

The first-born should be named after the father's family. That's the way it is done, and that's the way we're going to do it.

Now to hear Theodosios raise his usually meek voice certainly caused a little surprise, but not half as much as Vaia's retort.

8

Your family . . . Ha . . . What claims has your family
got? Your mother was a whore . . . a Turkish whore
at that . . . and your father, why he's nothing but a
common . . .

Vaia was round and fat with a baby and Theodosios
was hard and brown from working in the sun; and then
he pushed her, and he pushed her, and maybe that's
why the baby turned out to be hairy like a gorilla. To
give birth to a child hairy like a gorilla, you will agree,
is a very sad thing. After the child was born, yiayia
Stella crossed herself. She wondered what could have
brought this terrible matiasma upon their house.

Someone has surely given us the evil eye. This must
be kept within the family.

But by the afternoon of that very same day every
man, woman and child of the village had heard of the
baby gorilla; that's the sort of village this was. It was
the sort of village where every mother had to carry her
child five miles from the Zandelli hospital, with the
blood on the walls, to the village. She had to carry it
over the bridge and there hand it over to its father. And
all the villagers gathered on the foot of the bridge to
see the child and as they kissed it, one at a time, they
would say, Ah what a beautiful child! May it live for a
hundred years. Then there was singing and dancing. If
the child were fatherless, like those of the village

whores, then the whore's own father or perhaps her brother would come to collect the child. And the villagers would still come to say, Ah what a beautiful child! May it live for a hundred years. Then there was singing and dancing. And if the child were born without legs or arms, or even without a head, then the mother would leave the child at the foot of the bridge. The villagers would let out their pigs which would maul and eat the child. Professional mourners were brought to cry and beat their breasts and, if the weather permitted, a hog would be slaughtered and roasted. The people would sing and dance to the rising smell of burning pig's blood.

With her gorilla child in her arms Vaia set off from the Zandelli hospital with the blood on the walls. The weather was warm for this time of year. Good tobacco weather. But the gorilla child was so big and heavy, such a burden really; not what she had longed for. It looked a lot like her father in-law. It was wrong, all wrong; not what she had longed for at all. She would be up to the spring amidst the rocks soon. Maybe she could smash its ugly little head against the rocks and take a refreshing drink. It didn't cry either. Unnatural that was, all babies cried.

But Vaia did not stop. She wasn't really thirsty, and besides, she wanted to get to the bridge. The village elders would be there, her husband would be there, and they would decide its fate. But when she reached the bridge, no one was there, not a single soul. No one had known what to do—not the elders, not the women, not the children, not the Turks, not her parents, and especially not her husband. So they all stayed home and locked their doors. But from the windows they were all watching, and in their houses they were all whispering. (Except for Theodosios who was lying in his field drunk on raki. As he slept, a field rat nibbled on his big toe, and he was so drunk he did not even feel it.) Vaia left the child at the foot of the bridge and began to walk across. All the villagers condemned her for being callous and hard-hearted. The child did not cry. She walked very slowly and waited. It let out one loud sob. She turned back, picked it up and carried it across, holding her head up high. All the villagers condemned her again, this time for bringing such an ill-omened child into the village. She walked through the empty streets to yiayia Stella's house and knocked on the door. When the door opened, Vaia said, Mother, I've come with my child. Yiayia Stella crossed herself and then took her daughter in. That was the last the villagers saw of her and her gorilla child for quite a while.

WHEN SOMETHING OR SOMEONE GOES MISSING HERE, THEY SAY THAT THE EARTH EATS

When something or someone goes missing here, they say that the earth eats. It is as if this is a hungry land which devours its people. The valley connected to the village was in fact once known as the Valley of Blood. The story goes that when the Turks came to take this village, there was a very fierce battle there. In this battle many Greeks were slaughtered. And even though that land was particularly fertile, none of the Greeks dared to use it. Only the Turkish families who lived on the outskirts of the village grew some corn, tomatoes, eggplants and beans there.

Once a Greek man, a very poor tinker called Pappatkas, went to the valley and found buried gold pieces. He began to boast his good luck. In the kafeneio he bought all the men raki and mezethes. At first Manolios the Kafedzis thought it was a joke and refused to serve the tinker, but he gladly obliged when he saw the sparkling gold pieces.

All the people soon heard about this gold and one by one they came to the kafeneio. Pappatkas continued buying raki for everyone. Soon the kafeneio was so full that no one else could fit through the door and the people who kept coming and coming had to be content standing outside the broad windows watching. The festivities went on for two days and two nights, and they would have gone on for even longer if Pappatkas had not decided he wanted a woman. Not just any woman. He was not satisfied with one of Mirella's Turkish gypsies. Pappatkas had always had a passion for Stefanos' wife, Meta.

The year the river flooded, destroying Turkish crops, was the year that Stefanos and his mother (who looked like a bull) first came to the village. It was rumoured he'd been a mercenary in Crete and was mixed up in bad business. He had very soft hands and was one of the few people in the village, apart from Mirella, who could read and write. People were very suspicious of him. The women of the village avoided him. At that time Meta's mother brought her to Mirella, and Meta was sold on the streets to keep her family alive. Meta was eleven and she was sold for a handful of corn.

Stefanos said he felt sorry for the tiny waif girl who hadn't even bled yet, so he bought her from her family for two pigs and a cow.

At Meta's wedding the Turkish crier sang a song warning mothers to protect their daughters' virtue from roosters. When Meta had been a child of perhaps four or five, she had sat on her balcony throwing stones at her family's rooster and swearing vicious curses at him. Meta had watched him mount their fourteen chickens.

What's he doing?
Why, he's ravishing them, laughed her father.

Meta had woken up one morning needing to piss. It was a hot morning with the sort of heat that makes you see things, but as she went to the outhouse she did not see the rooster. He flew onto her back and ripped off her nightshirt. As she ran to the outhouse, he mounted her again and with his claws tore her child's flesh. Locked up in the stinking toilet with the flies, naked body bleeding, she cried at the top of her lungs.

Ma . . . Ma . . . I've been ravished . . . The dirty dog, he's ravished me he has, he has.

The whole neighbourhood gathered around the outhouse. Her father broke down the door and carried her little body above his head as the villagers roared with laughter.

14

On her wedding day the eleven-year-old bride shivered uneasily as the crier sang. A tear slid down her face and she wiped it with her sleeve. No one seemed to notice as they drank and laughed, especially not her husband.

This nervous child always peeking behind her greasy black hair worked hard for her husband: in his fields, in his home and in his bed. She also looked after his huge mother who suffered from a peculiar paralysis which left her bed-ridden. And when her mother-in-law soiled her sheets, which was often and especially on cold nights, the dark waif girl could be seen standing in the snow scrubbing the sheets with ice and salt.

The Turks refused to look her in the eye, as she had married a Greek, and the Greeks took bets on how much longer she'd survive. They gave her eighteen months, but when they heard a dry cough it fell to six.

Meta survived those six months, and by the time she was thirty she'd had fourteen children and she'd become the biggest and most fierce woman the villagers had ever seen. She was the sort of woman who kept a clove of garlic under her tongue to sweeten her breath. It was said that her breast milk tasted of garlic, and this is most probably true, as her fourteen children never once fell ill despite the fact that they ran around in the snow all day.

She worked alone in her husband's fields. Planting, digging, picking, drying and selling the tobacco. And she nearly always got the best price, not only because her crop was of such good quality but also because the merchants knew better than to try to cheat her. Once one had tried and under a false pretence she lured him to the middle of the field in the middle of the night and there she thumped him on the head so hard his eyeballs fell out. And even though the man went blind, he refused to testify against her. Though no one actually congratulated her, secretly all the villagers rejoiced. This merchant had robbed many families of their livelihood, leaving them to starve.

If the crops did fail, as was occasionally bound to happen, she would put on her husband's black and grey striped breeches and go hunting in the valley (being Turkish she was allowed there). Meta would never take a weapon on these hunting trips. With her bare hands she would kill wild boars, breaking their jaws open. (Boar meat is very tough but also quite nutritious.) She would wrestle with wolves, strangle them and skin them, bringing back warm blankets for her children.

When the villagers saw Meta walking down the cobbled streets dragging dead boars and wolf skins behind her, the women would automatically cross themselves and the men would spit on the ground. But the truth was that secretly all the men had a burning passion for Meta. A desire that they would never admit to but that none the less made them go weak at the knees and muddled in the brain every time they saw her. And the more pious and righteous the men claimed to be, and

16

the louder they cursed the Turkish beast, the greater was their desire. (In fact, Mirella's house had a scandalous cure for impotence. The whores would enter the bed chamber having rubbed garlic oil between their legs.)

Shame began to grow in Stefanos' heart. Meta was his. He had bought her lawfully for two pigs and now every idiot in the village had a secret claim to her. Stefanos woke up every night screaming because he dreamt that his blood was turning to water. Meta would make him a warm cup of chamomile to comfort him. At some point Stefanos had lost control of her. She had grown and grown so that, it seemed to him, his house could not contain her any longer. In the early days he had panicked and tried to control her. The kitchen was warm with the smell of steaming green beans.

You are an uneducated Turkish dog, a stupid animal. You are worth nothing. Do you hear? Anyone could have had you, and I saved you. I saved you.

Meta turned around, knocked him to the floor and, holding him down, stuck cloves of garlic up the orifices of his body till he lost consciousness. She then went to the shed by the fields and made a punching bag out of a sack of wheat and practised her boxing till dusk. Stefanos was found unconscious by his youngest son, but after the cloves of garlic were removed he made a full recovery, except for a ruined eardrum.

Now, having become the richest man in the village, Pappatkas set his heart on Meta. So all the celebrations followed him up the street to Stefanos' house. It was Meta herself who opened the door. And the crowd cheered as he handed her three gold pieces, and she took him in, shutting the door behind him. The women went home to feed their children. The men (except for the Ten Pious Men, of course, who left the party somewhat disgusted) stayed outside the front of the house all night singing songs about brave warriors deflowering virgin brides. This continued till the sun rose on the village houses. When there was a stirring at the front door the men began to cheer loudly but stopped when they saw it was only Stefanos. They jeered and threw stones at him before he even had a chance to open his mouth. Then Meta came out on the balcony with a pot of boiling water and threatened to pour it over their heads.

You can all go home, she said. The old snake you're waiting for left through the back way last night. Your singing and jeering have kept my poor children up all night. You can all just go home and let my children get some sleep.

Meta tipped the pot and the crowd scattered.

When Pappatkas went missing, the good people of the village shook their heads. Ah the earth eats, they said. It serves him right for upturning the soil of the Valley of Blood.

But there was another rumour which could be traced back to the Ten Pious Men. It said that Meta herself had murdered Pappatkas, stolen the gold, and in the night dragged his body to the valley and threw it in the river. This rumour caught on surprisingly fast. The Ten Pious Men volunteered to risk their lives in an attempt to bring Meta to justice. They set about making a trap. Meta must have sensed that something was in the air because she spent a lot of time down at the shed practising her boxing. The trap was a monstrous device made of steel and spears. It was set in the fields. Meta found it. The Ten Pious Men, fearing for their lives, went into hiding. But Meta took the trap home in high spirits. Rather pleased with herself, she painted it a golden yellow and hung it up in the courtyard.

Now that should have been the end of that. The sensible people agreed that what happened next should never have happened. But as the Ten Pious Men came out of hiding one by one, they could be seen in dark corners and at dark times whispering with Stefanos. It was on a very dark morning indeed that Stefanos stole into his sleeping wife's room with a black rooster. He let it loose upon her. And it was in that strange realm which is neither of the sleeping world nor of the waking that she let out one soundless scream. If you have heard a soundless scream, you will know that it is enough to wither your soul. But Stefanos did not hear it, he closed the door behind him. And when the Ten Pious Men came with their spears and heavy rope they waited anxiously outside the door till the sun rose and the cock crowed. When they burst into the room there was no need for spears or heavy rope. Meta lay on the floor, smaller than the child bride bought for two pigs and a cow, and even smaller than the child whore bought for a handful of corn. The cock sat pecking on her head. She kept repeating something in Turkish which, try as he did, Stefanos could not make out above the clicking noise her tongue made in her dry mouth.

It was very gently by the hand that Stefanos led his wife out of the village to the Zandelli prison where they locked her up for many years. Pappatkas was never found dead or alive, and neither was the gold. As for the Ten Pious Men, they prospered surprisingly well for a few years to come. Stefanos neglected his children and the cultivation of his fields and took up digging (if it were not for the kindness of neighbouring women, his children would have starved). After the autumn rains (autumn being the season when leaves fall and dreams are forever lost) he would wander about in the mud at the foot of the mountain, searching for the bones and treasures of the great Macedonian Kings. It was at about this time that he began to lose his sense of direction and walked about the village streets for hours, unable to find his way home. People would take pity on him

20

and send their children to walk him to his house. As for his own children, the younger ones forgot their real mother altogether, and with misty eyes Stefanos told them stories of a mother with amazing powers. Among these was the ability to transform herself into any animal she wished (with the exception of a black cock). For the rest of his life Theodosios actually believed that he had been suckled by a goat with fourteen nipples.

That was the story of Meta, the fiercest woman in the village and the mother of Theodosios. Now you must not completely forget her there in her jail, for where the merchant's eyeballs fell and soaked into the earth a seed began to grow. A seed of an olive tree. And when this olive tree breaks the surface and grows tall, Meta returns.

NOW IT IS ABOUT TIME TO TELL YOU WHAT HAPPENED TO THE GORILLA CHILD

Now it is about time to tell you what happened to the gorilla child. It was six months since its birth, and no one in the village had seen it. Ah, the earth eats, they said. Some suspected that such a monstrous baby would surely have died and was perhaps already buried in the courtyard under the orange tree. Others doubted its existence altogether, as if it had been just a tale told by a story-teller with a sick sense of humour. Every night the neighbours cleaned the wax from their ears, and, with their heads against the wall, they listened. But all they heard was the chattering of the family and, on some nights, Vaia weeping.

It was generally agreed that this was a time of great difficulty for Vaia. People were very sympathetic towards her, and they spoke harshly of Theodosios who never went to see her again. If he saw Vaia out in the street, he would quickly cross to the other side. People also noticed that Theodosios began to work very hard. He cultivated the fields by the hillside which had been left mostly untouched since his mother's imprisonment. He would also wake up very early in the morning, ride down to the marsh and load the mule with thick reeds which he would use to weave mats. These mats fetched good prices at the Sunday-morning bazaars. To be fair on him, it must be said that every week he would send his earnings to his wife and every week she would smell the package, lick it cautiously, and send it back unopened.

But, contrary to what the villagers thought, this time was one of the happiest periods of Vaia's life. When she turned back, picked up her child and saved its life, it was as if she had saved her own. She became totally oblivious to the rest of the world and spent every living moment with her child. Yiayia Stella and pappous Yiorgos did not like to look at the child, for its face reminded them of a monkey's, and they mourned it as if it were already dead. But despite this, they went to great lengths for their monstrous grandchild. Yiayia Stella baked apples, knitted colourful baby clothes and would sneak out and buy pretty little brushes from the gypsies. Pappous Yiorgos cleaned out the upstairs room which had been left untouched for more than twenty years since his brother Nestor (who plays a twisted part in this tale) had run off with the gypsies. Pappous Yiorgos wondered why he had never done this before.

He burnt all his brother's clothes in the stone bread-
oven. Yiayia Stella wore black that day and stayed
inside. When pappous Yiorgos turned around, he saw
his daughter standing there with her child held against
her hip, staring intently into the fire. Vaia said that the
burning clothes smelt horrible. She could not understand why they just did not give them away to some
poor gypsies.

And for months afterwards pappous Yiorgos could
not eat bread from that oven because he thought it smelt
of his brother. He never told anyone about this, but
that's when he decided to build the six-foot wall around
the house.

Don't be a fool, his wife said. We're much to busy for
silly things like that. Vaia won't be in the fields this
year, and we can't rely on that good-for-nothing son-
in-law.

Pappous Yiorgos did not believe that their grandchild
could live to see its first birthday, yet he convinced his
wife that it was necessary to build this wall so that Vaia
would not be afraid to let the baby play outside. It
needed sunshine so its bones would not grow crooked.
The yiayia could not possibly argue against this. So the
wall was built. This is part of the reason why for so
long the villagers never saw the child.

But Vaia fed him, talked to him, played with him,
slept with him on her breast, and she bathed with him.   24

That one hour in the bathtub came to replace her childish dreams of heaven, which had up to then been of bread dripping honey and ravenous pigs consuming masses of apples.

Vaia always took special care to obey the little rules. In this village it is an old custom that women who have recently given birth must always veil their faces when going to the well, or else the trees will dry up. As such a lyhouna, Vaia had a special veil made for her face, and she always wore it. For this she was highly commended.

Every day she would draw water, light the fire, boil the water, fill the tub. She lay in the water until it got cold, with the gorilla child against her breast. She was thrilled by the contrast in their bodies. Hers so white, so smooth that it seemed to glow in the dark, and her child's so hairy and black. Then there was just the pleasure of brushing his hair and delousing him. In fact one could say that she was in love with his very monstrosity. Sometimes she would lie in the tub till it got dark. The water became cold but the child was so warm; the child kept the mother warm.

Yiayia Stella and pappous Yiorgos went to sleep and in the dark yiayia Stella would open her eyes and hear the 'bloomm bloomm bloomm bloomm' of the water hitting against the tub. She would wake up confused. She would think there was a storm. Sometimes she would think the river of the Valley of Blood was flood-

25

ing. Then she would hear her daughter crying in her bed, and yiayia Stella would be relieved.

The deep sobs were not something Stella understood, they were not understandable; they were in fact unknowable, yet they were familiar and comforting. Vaia was not crying for her gorilla child, nor was she crying for the uncertainty of her future or any trauma from her past. Yiayia Stella could see that this was the happiest time in her daughter's life. Vaia's sadness came well before her lifetime. Vaia's sadness was the old sadness.

Yiayia Stella knew that her parents' bones would be glowing warm in their box on the mantelpiece. She had heard her own mother crying those very same tears, and at the time she had thought it was because the old mother's life had been so hard. She had thought that her mother cried because she had two invalid daughters whom no one would marry. Stella thought her mother had cried because the silkworms did not spin cocoons or because their family was so poor.

When she grew up, Stella herself had cried these very same tears, sobbed till it became unbearable. Then one day Stella came to know that there was nothing exclusive about this sadness, that sadness does not belong to us, it is totally, absolutely impersonal. With this she found a calm pleasure, and at the age of twenty-one her hair turned grey overnight.

Both her parents died during the blood-pissing epidemic. When their bones were exhumed, as is the tradition in these parts, she had washed them lovingly but refused to put them in the bone room. She had placed them in a black box that resembled a giant silkworm box and kept it on the mantelpiece. When the old sadness came upon her, often at night after she had made love to her husband, she would sneak out to the shed with the box of bones. Laying them out on a wheat sack, she would watch them glow warm like red coals in the dark. She would try to separate her mother's skeleton from her father's. Then she would hug the bones against her body until she was relieved of this sadness and the bones grew cold again. She would then pack them away and return to her bed.

In the church cabinet, which has always been reserved for precious things, there are two stones. These are the stones that St. Vaia had used to grind wheat. When Agha Emred burnt the village down, many years ago, and everyone fled to the mountain, the two small grinding stones were the only things belonging to his wife that Stellios saved. Stellios the Eminent Citizen fled to the mountains with two grinding stones and his baby daughter. When he found out about the gruesome death of his wife, he put these stones in the cabinet for precious things. His daughter, who was to be called Despina after his own mother, he renamed Vaia, after his slaughtered wife.

When this Vaia grew up, she would talk about the Great Fire as if she remembered it. She would even swear on her mother's grave (this was a serious oath, since her mother was made a saint) that from the hidden caves in the mountain she had seen the light of the fire. But she was only days old when Agha Emred sent his squabbling sons to set the village on fire. It seems more likely that what she remembered was the return. Playing in the dust and rubble with Nikolios and his brothers, the taste of ash, the smell of white-wash and the feverish state of the re-building.

This Vaia grew up with the original spirit of the rebuilding. As she sat at the loom weaving she would make up songs about the camels of the Agha drinking at the well, about the revolt, about the fire, about love and freedom. She would sing at the top of her voice as if the past and the future were hers; the roots of her black hair and her beautiful golden body were always speckled with whitewash from the rebuilding.

This was a time when the people were a bit crazy from freedom and starvation. When Vaia's father, Stellios the Eminent Citizen, suggested that he go into the big town to bring back wondrous new ways of doing things, the people did not laugh. When he asked them all to give him one gold coin from their family collection, they did not hesitate. When he left there was a great day of feasting and the priest blessed Stellios. There was nothing to eat in the village and so they asked Mirella to prepare something. With her strange herbs Mirella could cook anything. She prepared a feast of boiled bitter grass and turtle meat. No one was unsatisfied by the feasting. When the people gathered at the bridge and watched Stellios riding away with two starving horses and a termite-ridden carriage, no one suspected that he might not reach his destination. When six months passed and they had heard nothing of him, no one doubted that he was on his way. When six years passed and he did not return, they prepared for his imminent return. His daughter still sang as she wove at the loom, as if the past and the future were hers. Even though the village was always on the brink of starvation, no one actually died of hunger.

One woman ate her mother-in-law, but this was out of desperation. Her mother-in-law had sent her to the river to wash the wool, telling her not to come back till that wool was white. This woman went to the river and scrubbed and scrubbed till her fingers froze but the wool was still filthy. In a moment of desperation she asked God and the Blessed Saints to take pity on her and turn her into a bear. Perhaps there was some mischievous spirit, some kallikandsaros crossing her path, for the woman was instantly transformed into a big brown bear. The woman ran back home and ate her mother-in-law. The bear was later seen heading towards the mountain. Such was the spirit of the age that no

29

one was sent to kill the bear. It was just part of the mystery of that house.

When Stellios returned sixteen years later in the same carriage but drawn by stronger horses, no one was the least bit surprised. Nor were they discouraged when all he had to show for these sixteen years and two hundred and fifty gold coins was one skinny Englishman named Robert Charles Salter and two hundred and fifty little black boxes. This was the beginning of the silkworm.

Robert Charles Salter was a sailor who claimed to have been in many of the infamous sea battles against the Turks. He claimed to be a lover of Greeks, of antiquity, and to be an expert in the raising of silkworms. In the kafeneio he told stories of the battles in which he fought. Everyone gathered to hear him. Sometimes, to thrill the villagers, he took his shirt off and showed them images of ships and serpents which were etched into his back.

Everyone got a little black box full of eggs. Under the directions of Robert Charles Salter they laid the eggs on mats of mulberry leaves. They watched the worms eat and spin their cocoons. Robert Charles Salter, who dressed in motley coloured patches and wore an earring in each ear, strutted about like a wizard.

At the kafeneio Robert Charles Salter and Vaia always danced together. Of course, as they were unrelated and unmarried, they always held a handkerchief between them. But everyone noticed that she had a way

30

of dancing which would twist the kerchief so that her fingers would always be touching his. When Robert Charles Salter was overcome by one of his terrible toothaches, Vaia made him special compresses out of bread soaked in raki and cracked pepper. When she baked bread, she would always leave little buns which Robert Charles Salter spread with the fig jam that Vaia also made specially for him.

Every morning, before she went to collect mulberry leaves, she tied her best kerchief around her head, washed her face with goat's milk, her hair in rosemary water, and scrubbed her teeth with salt. She continued to sing about the camels of the Agha, as if the past and the future were hers.

But when the cocoons were nearly ready, Vaia was kidnapped by her neighbour Nikolios and his seven brothers. (Nikolios came from a very poor family, a family so poor that when the Ten Eminent Citizens began to allot the boxes of silkworms, his family got only half a box.) He took her to a shed in a neighbouring town, got very drunk, and raped her. He asked her to marry him. He kept her there for five days and she refused to speak or to eat a thing. When it looked as if she would die, Nikolios prepared to bring her home.

But then a messenger came from her father who had tracked her down. After all, by that very same day every man, woman and child of the village knew exactly what had happened. The messenger told her that the cocoons

31

had been fired and sold at excellent prices and there was plenty of food in the village. Her father said that if she did not want Nikolios, she should return to the village and he would try to find her a husband. This was more than most fathers would do for a ruined daughter. But this Vaia was too proud to return to the village unmarried. She did not want to marry some old widower.

Locked up for five days without food, she came to understand that time is not as she had always imagined it to be. She lost sight of the past, of her mother the saint. She lost sight of the future, of her father the Eminent Citizen. She thought only of the woman who turned into a bear. So that is how it was. At any present moment one was a woman scrubbing wool by the river, with a woman's thoughts and a woman's past and a woman's future. The next moment one was a bear. Vaia tried to force the tale out of her mind in case she might turn into a bear. For at this moment to have to eat Nikolios was more distasteful than to have to make love to him.

On the sixth night she ate a full plate of bean stew and even asked for another piece of bread to wipe her plate clean. That night Nikolios and this Vaia were married. On the seventh day they returned to the village amidst great celebrations with the money that came from the silkworm. Vaia twitched her nose at the unfamiliar smell. It was the smell of burning pig fat. A smell

32

that had not been smelled in the village for many years. Robert Charles Salter had left in her absence. People smiled when they heard her say that she hoped he would be shipwrecked, that she hoped he would drown and that his body would be mauled by a school of dogfish. And, according to the histories of Stefanos, this is exactly what happened to him.

People said that this Vaia lived a good life with Nikolios. She spent most of her life working on the silkworm. Nikolios was in awe of her. He could only make love to her when he was drunk. There were three daughters born from these lustful bouts. The first was half-deaf, the second fully mute and the third, Stella, with perfect senses, but her hair did turn grey overnight at the age of twenty-one.

PROSPERITY GOES IN WAVES

Prosperity goes in waves, so when things are going well the villagers feast and sing, but always they wait for fortunes to change. They even have a name for this. They call it matiasma. It can happen to a whole village which can in one instance be thrown from prosperity into disease, or it can happen to an individual person. When people compliment others, they spit afterwards, as if they are spitting their words out. For if the devil or even just a kallikandsaros is crossing your path while you are being complimented, then you might be matiased.

When things began to go wrong in the village, the people just accepted that prosperity went in waves. First the wines went sour. The barrels appeared absolutely air-tight. People even painted them with melted wax to ensure this. But this did not save them. In the night the wine from a certain barrel was good and by morning it was sour. After your first barrel went, one by one all your barrels were lost. Even though the Turks were not 34

immune to this, people blamed the Turks. They blamed
the gypsies and they blamed pregnant women. Finally
people poured barrel after barrel down the river till the
streams were flowing red. Two bulls drank from a
puddle of still waters downstream and went crazy
through the village. Before they were shot, they impaled
two old pappouthes who for the last twenty years had
met on the seats in the town square every Sunday
morning to tell each other dirty jokes about naked Casia
chasing her white chickens. When their trampled bodies
were collected, the villagers were shocked to see smiles
on their faces. (If a person dies with a smile on their
face this is because they intend to take someone else
with them.)

On hot afternoons when the villagers slept, snakes
came down through the thatched roofs of the sheds and
suckled the udders of sleeping ewes till they drew
blood. In June the silkworms did not spin cocoons. They
ate and ate mulberry leaves till they got fat and white,
and then they all died. By the end of June temperatures
soared and the earth stank with the stench of dead
silkworm and the sourness of bad wine. So when the
summer rains came the villagers rejoiced that the earth
would be cleansed. But unlike the summer rains which
last for a day or two, the rain which started in July beat
down until August. The tobacco crop turned black. The
river once again flooded in the valley, ruining Turkish
crops. The udders of ewes dropped off in women's

hands as they tried to milk them. Even the eels in the marsh died and floated to the surface of the water.

Theodosios would wake up every morning, wipe the fog from the window and watch the rain falling and know all his hard work was amounting to nothing. He would still weave his mats but there was no bazaar on Sunday mornings. When he had no money to send to his wife, he began to fret. The first time he had sent an old kerchief which had belonged to his mother Meta. Vaia wrinkled her nose curiously and had to lick it twice to understand what it was. She sent it back. The next week Theodosios put two dried figs into the package. Again Vaia wrinkled her nose curiously but this time she opened the package and ate the figs.

Theodosios was quite frightened and thought the parcel may have been lost. The next week he sent Vaia some dried apricots, and when they did not return he was pleased. So Theodosios stopped thinking about his ruined crop and at night he lay awake thinking about what little delicacy he would send his wife. Other than his father who enjoyed digging when the heavy rains subsided, Theodosios must have been one of the few people who had found some sort of pleasure in the rains. The truth is that he was even a little afraid of what might happen when the rain stopped. (What happened was that on the first Sunday bazaar he traded all the mats he had woven during the rains for a whole sack of dried banana chips.)

36

It was during these rains that Theodosios' father Stefanos found the Mud Man. Twice he nearly drowned before he found the slushy black remains of a man who Stefanos insisted was the first general of Alexander the Great. The Priest of Casia and the Elders of the village refused Stefanos' demand to preserve the body (with herbs, salt and oil, like a pickle) and to keep it in the cabinet with St. Vaia's grinding stones. Remembering the smiling faces of the two old pappouthes impaled by the bulls, they insisted that the body should be buried to avoid disease. The body was given a holy burial, but the priest and Elders would not engrave the name of Alexander the Great's first general on the tombstone. Instead they wrote

The Mud Man.

One night, soon after, during a terrible electric storm, two brothers, the sons of an Elder, stole into the yard and engraved a new inscription on the stone,

General Pappatkas.

The next morning the rains stopped and the grave-yard smelt of singed hair. Both brothers had identical black burns running from the centre of their scalps to the bridge of their noses. Both boys had died with smiles on their faces. The villagers shivered when Meriklis the Grave-digger told them this. Even though the rains had stopped, the deaths had not.

The church bells rang. After the burial, people began to gather in the village square. Manolios the Kafedzis set up tables and served raki and mezethes. The Turkish crier sang to Allah and the people came. Some mourned the death of loved ones; others talked about how they would survive the winter. But most people just waited for something to happen. Then the debate began. The Great Debate between the Priest of Casia and the Blind Traveller.

The Priest of Casia said, we must look into our village to see what is causing this terrible matiasma. The Elders said, we must search for it and weed it out. Some people cheered. The Turks waited to hear exactly what was to be weeded out. The women objected. Prosperity comes in waves and, left by themselves, things certainly come right, they said. The Priest of Casia said, there is one family in the village which has not suffered the losses of the rest. And the simple people began to stamp their feet and cry out, Who?

The house of Yiorgos Liaris, cried an Elder.

It was true that in the house of pappous Yiorgos and yiayia Stella everyone was of very good health, their wines were of superb flavour and it had actually been a fine year for the silkworm. As for their ewes, they not only kept their udders but gave lots of milk so that pappous Yiorgos milked them three times a day. Yiayia Stella made cheese which she gave to orphan children. Even their chickens laid twice a day. Pappous Yiorgos had been very careful not to boast of his good fortune. 38

He had brought the silkworm merchant in through the back way. Pappous Yiorgos was the only person in the village with cocoons to sell. And their tobacco plants that year had been tall and green. People now began to wonder what was happening behind that wall.

The Priest of Casia roared that it was the family of pappous Yiorgos which had brought the matiasma upon them. There was another moment of silence.

Then came the laughter. A laughter which started off like an excited scream of a child and then gained momentum and depth until it was like a song sung by someone very old who had waited for a lifetime to sing it. Instantly the people were reminded of the smiling corpses. The women crossed themselves. What supernatural, what positively demonic power could make such a sound? Only an old man came forward, tap, tap, tapping with his stick. A blind traveller, or so he had appeared at first glance. He said,

Can someone tell me, this gorilla child, what family is he from?

The people went dumb. The truth is that the gorilla child had been something so unnatural that it had not been accepted in the minds of the people. This moment was confusing and it was Pourthitsa's son, the Village Idiot, who stumbled forward (he could not help stumbling for his left leg was partially withered and two inches shorter than his right). He blurted out,

Why, he's the son of Theodosios and grandson of Stefanos and Yiorgos.

The village shuddered at this litany and immediately began to chatter and spit as if awakened from an uneasy sleep.

It is this ill-omened grandchild of pappous Yiorgos . . .

The Priest's voice echoed high above the mountain as it had never done before. The Priest of Casia stopped in mid-sentence and looked around, a little frightened. Then he gained courage and thundered.

. . . this monstrosity of pappous Yiorgos has brought the matiasma upon us.

The people held their breath. The Blind Traveller moved towards the Priest and as he spoke his physical person changed before their very eyes. This change did not just happen once, it was happening continuously. Just by lightly tilting his head, the old man's lips became full and his eyes softened so that the villagers could have sworn that they were actually looking at a woman. But then he would move his face up towards the sun and he was a man again, and at this point there was a defiance in his body which was certainly over one hundred years old.

He argued eloquently. If prosperity went in waves, then surely this family had been spared disaster because

40

of their previous misfortune in giving birth to such a child. At this point he talked of recent events of the village as if he had always lived there and, though he had appeared at first as a stranger, for a moment he became familiar. He was someone they had known all their lives, so familiar that the villagers were at the point of calling out his name, but then he changed again. And he was a total stranger to them.

The Priest of Casia yelled that what was needed was the sacrifice of the gorilla child.

The Blind Traveller began to change colour. First his skin darkened and his eyes grew beady. Even the shape of his face was altered. He was turning into a gypsy, into a Turk. So all the Turks leaned forward to see and they wondered who in the name of Allah was this person; the Greeks wondered what in the devil's name was it. The Elders wanted to tie him up and hold him down. The Priest of Casia wished him dead.

You dirty, diseased Turk. Who are you and what is your business here?

I am a blind traveller. My eyelids have become dry, so dry that they scrape against my eyes. I am looking for the mother of the gorilla child so I can wash my eyes with her milk and be comforted.

So they told him that Vaia was still living with her father, pappous Yiorgos, but before they could give him directions the Blind Traveller walked briskly up the street on exactly the right path. And the Village Idiot who had followed to show him the way was actually stumbling along behind him. The Blind Traveller began laughing joyfully, and then to everyone's amazement he began skipping up the street. From a distance people thought that he had changed into a goat. The Blind Traveller reached the house with the six-foot wall, knocked on the door, and yiayia Stella answered it.

Now, there was once a Vaia who had died in her sleep. This was Stella's first child. Really this all began when Stella's hair turned grey and she found herself swamped with suitors. Grey hair was so very becoming to her, people said that she looked like an angel. Poor Pourthitsa the Matchmaker was run off her feet. In the end, Stella decided to make her choice from the two Liaris brothers because they had cousins willing to marry her two sisters. (One sister being half-deaf and the other fully mute, it was not easy to find husbands for sisters like these.)

The two Liaris brothers were named Nestor and Yiorgos and you could never think of one without the other. Everyone always thought of them as Nestor and Yiorgos, always in that order. Though Nestor was younger he was stronger and taller than his brother. Yiorgos was short and stumpy. His upper torso was of a good size, but his limbs were small as if he were meant to have grown taller but never did. People said this was

42

the very case. They said the mother loved the younger son more and would always take food from the elder son's plate to feed the younger son.

Nestor was born unexpectedly on the kitchen floor. When everyone was rushing about preparing for his birth, his older sister Pawonia grabbed Yiorgos and locked him outside the house. Yiorgos was three years old. He leaned up against the window and watched his brother being born. He decided there and then to kill him. Many times he picked him up and lay him under the horse so that it might trample him. But the mother always saved Nestor. To make Yiorgos love his brother she put sugar cubes in the baby's nappies.

Come Yiorgos, see what your brother's got for you. He shits sugar for you.

And so eventually Yiorgos abandoned his plans to kill Nestor. Instead he nursed his brother with great care. When Nestor was old enough to walk, Yiorgos followed him wherever he went. As young boys the two brothers ate their meals together. And it was Yiorgos himself who took all the meat, in fact anything good from his plate, and put it on his brother's, leaving only pieces of cabbage floating on his own plate. But despite this affection, when Nestor grew barely tall enough to reach his brother he would jump up, grab his hair and smack him in the face.

As they grew older the difference in their characters

became more and more apparent to the villagers. Whereas Yiorgos was a gentle, kind man who enjoyed the company of children, Nestor was mean and rough, and if any children got in his way he kicked dust in their faces. He only ever referred to his older brother as that ugly little cripple.

Nestor was a handsome man, a great dancer. The women of the village whispered that he had sweet blood. But this is all they did, just whisper. For no woman who respected herself would be seen with Nestor. The only women of this village who had anything to do with him were the whores. It is well known that his father gave him the best fields, which should rightfully have gone to the eldest son, and Nestor squandered these in the brothel. There were girls from other villages where his reputation had not yet reached who followed him home. When he was through with them he dumped them in the streets.

Then the fathers and the brothers came to the village to take the ruined girls home. Sometimes they came to kill Nestor. Everyone gathered to watch Nestor fight the fathers and the brothers of the ruined girls. Glasses were shattered, chairs broken and tables smashed but Nestor never lost a fight in his life. Nestor was much too fast and much too strong. And he owed Manolios the Kafedzis a fortune in broken furniture.

As for Yiorgos, he never got into any fights, and he tagged along behind Nestor, watching his brother's

44

women from far away. Sometimes he cleaned up the ruined girls and paid for a carriage to take them home. Whatever Yiorgos, who was sensible and gentle, thought of Nestor's ugly ways, it was also plain to see that he still adored his younger brother.

But everything changed when Nestor fell in love with Stella. He stopped going to the brothel. He stopped drinking and he stopped fighting. He spent his days singing wonderful songs outside her house. The villagers could hardly believe it. To help his brother, Yiorgos left bundles of fish wrapped in cloth outside Stella's door. Nestor was embarrassed that his brother would leave smelly fish outside the door of an angel.

The day the entire village was waiting for finally came. Pourthitsa the Matchmaker went to the Liaris household to tell them that Stella had decided to marry. However, it was not Nestor that she wanted but Yiorgos.

The entire village was outraged with Stella because, despite his ways, they had adored Nestor. As if to defend her choice, Stella said that when he went fishing in the marsh, Yiorgos always knew where the fish were. She thought that always to know where the fish are and always to be able to catch them was an excellent trait in a husband.

When Yiorgos married Stella, Nestor said he would kill him on his wedding day. Nestor got drunk in the kafeneio and said he would kill them both. And the

45

whole village turned up to the wedding expecting one brother to slaughter the other. But nothing like this happened. When the wedding was over, Nestor went back to his bad habits. His whoring and drinking were even worse than before.

Now after she was married, and after her invalid sisters were married, Stella had refused to abandon her family house, so Yiorgos went to live with her. In these parts often the bride will go to live with the husband's family, unless his family is very poor. But Stella would not leave the house that had belonged to her parents. Stella's father-in-law said that if she were going to split his household like this and take one of his working sons from him, then she would also have to take one of his younger children to feed. Every day the old man sent one of the children to her. Every day Stella would send the child and his things straight back to his father.

One evening Nestor lost a fight. Two men came from a distant town and cut him up badly. Everyone watched but no one tried to help him. Manolios the Kafedzis told him to settle his account before the end of the month. Nestor packed up his things and went to Stella's house. At first Stella wanted to send him away but Yiorgos said they could not turn his younger brother out like that. And so Nestor came to live with the couple.

The gossips said many things. They said it was not right for one woman to be living alone with two brothers who had both been her suitors. They said it was not right for Stella to have both the working sons of her father-in-law (Nestor worked a lot harder on Stella's fields than he had ever done on his father's). Others said that the devious old man had sent Nestor there on purpose to disrupt the house of his daughter-in-law.

That year, instead of growing silkworms, Stella put everything into the tobacco crop. She had very little money because she had given most of it as dowry for her two sisters' marriages. But she had lots of land and both the working sons of her father-in-law. No one in the village had grown tobacco on such a large scale before. They thought that she was mad. If the crops failed she would lose everything; the money-lenders would take her house and her land. She would have to go to live in her father-in-law's house. Many people thought, secretly even hoped, that she would fail.

But Stella knew something that the gossips did not know. She knew that Nestor had not come to the house for her. She knew that Nestor came to the house because he could not live without Yiorgos. She understood this, and everything in the house went well, until Nestor saw Stella with the bones.

It was only by accident that he saw her six months pregnant in her calico nightdress, sobbing as she clutched the glowing bones against her. He was so disturbed by this image that he lay awake at nights just sweating and waiting for the sound of her footsteps.

When she went into the shed with the bones he too came down and stood by the window watching.

He did this many times until one night she saw his face in the window and went shrieking to her husband. That very night, much to the satisfaction of the gossips, the two brothers fought out in the street. Yiorgos was not quite sure why he was fighting his brother, and after the fight the window of the shed was nailed up and Nestor returned to live with the couple again.

It was humiliating to Stella that Nestor had seen her with the bones. Yiorgos just continued to adore his brother as if nothing had happened. The two brothers often stayed up late and talked about Stella's crops and her baby. And in some way that she could not understand, something had changed between the three of them, and for Stella living in that house had become unbearable. But she put everything aside because the harvest was coming. Nestor was a lot stronger and faster than her husband. He was needed for the harvest.

Stella never spoke to Nestor again. In fact she did not speak to anyone during this time. Her whole body began to swell and turn red like a plum. She stopped speaking to her child. (Before she had spent hours sitting under the orange tree stroking her belly and chatting with her unborn daughter.) She stopped embracing her parents' bones. She only went to the fields early in the morning and spoke to the tobacco plants, entreating them to grow and grow. People began

48

to laugh at her. The swelling was so bad that Nestor and Yiorgos told her to stay in bed but she just would not hear of it. Yiorgos prayed to St. Vaia, he was so terrified that his young wife would die. Nestor worked like a mule so that Stella's crop would grow.

Stella gave birth in the fields. She had not spoken to the child in her for months. She felt this child was a stranger to her and she wanted to bury her in the field where they buried the placenta. Take this child away from me. That is what Stella said to her husband. Yiorgos and Nestor came and took the child away. Even though the first-born is usually named after the father's side, Nestor and Yiorgos decided that they should call the child Vaia, after Stella's mother.

Their crop that year stood out from the surrounding fields. They got the best price not only in the village but in the whole district. So Stella stayed in her house. But the child who was born in the fields died in its sleep, hours after its birth.

Stella's father-in-law called his son Nestor to his house and asked Nestor what happened to his grandchild. Nestor lost his temper and broke things in his father's house. He told his father that it was not *his grandchild*; the child was hers, only hers. It looked just like her. He described the child to them. He said it had huge black eyes, just like hers. He said the child was an angel and then he buried his face in the palms of

49

his huge hands and cried. That night he left the village with a troop of gypsies and he never returned.

The crops of Stella and Yiorgos continued to prosper and, four years later, Stella had another child whom they named Vaia after their first child. That day Yiorgos went to the kafeneio and paid off his brother's debt. Manolios the Kafedzis wanted more money because the payment was so late. Yiorgos threw his money on the table. Before he left he said, Manolios I don't know how a miser like yourself ever became a kafedzis. When he got home he was in a foul mood, and he asked his wife why Nestor had run off like that. Stella said that everything always happens for the best and she told him about a decision she had taken after the death of their first child. She had decided that she should reject nothing and no one in life. That there is always a place in the back of one's heart or a corner of one's house even for the things one fears most. Two deep lines formed on Stella's forehead after she took this decision.

So when the Blind Traveller knocked on her door wanting to cleanse his eyes with her daughter's breast milk, yiayia Stella took him in.

THE BLIND TRAVELLER SAT IN THE COURTYARD WITH PAPPOUS YIORGOS LISTENING TO NEWS OF RECENT DISASTERS

The Blind Traveller sat in the courtyard with pappous Yiorgos listening to news of recent disasters and chewing on slabs of Turkish Delight. Occasionally his lips curled slightly until his teeth showed and his expression could have been mistaken for a smile. He asked no questions. He just nodded his head. When pappous Yiorgos asked where he was from and where he was going, he replied simply that he had come a long way. He laughed at this, that deep laughter which had disturbed the villagers so, and pappous Yiorgos watched him and was suddenly filled with desire and delight. (At this point he reached out to touch the traveller's face and then pulled his hand back again.) Yiayia Stella lingered in the courtyard as she cleaned out the stone oven listening, but hearing only laughter. Then she too began to get a ticklish chin and she laughed, gently at first. She tried to stop herself. She realised what a silly old woman she was just laughing for no reason at all. But it was no use. When she got the urge to guffaw, she stuck her head in the oven. When she pulled it out for air she was still laughing, and pappous Yiorgos went to her to wipe the black ash from her face, but they could not keep still long enough. He touched her, she guffawed, and they fell to the ground laughing.

Even though the Blind Traveller was not a relative, Vaia came downstairs with her gorilla child. In his presence the child cooed happily. The Blind Traveller wished to hold the child and as he ran his fingers against its fur the child began to screw up its face in such a way that Vaia was afraid it would shit on their guest. Yiayia Stella guessed that it was laughing. Vaia took the child from him. She fed the child. And then she stood over the Blind Traveller, his head back and his eyes open, she gently shook a drop of milk into each eye. The Blind Traveller thanked her warmly and after enjoying an evening meal of split peas and salted her-ring with the family, he spent the night with a blanket under the logs in the shed. The yiayia had offered him a room but he had insisted on the shed. Yiayia Stella thought he was a very humble man to sleep in the shed.

The Blind Traveller went on living with the family. He spent his days sitting on a log in the courtyard with a cane flyswatter, killing flies. Despite his blindness, he was an expert at this. The whitewash around the log was forever stained brown, and by noon the floor around the log was black with dead flies. For a couple of hours while everyone slept, the ants would come out and carry the flies away. When he woke, he would begin again. Sometimes in the evening he would mind the gorilla child when Vaia went to collect water. The gorilla child grew to love the Blind Traveller.

And then Pourthitsa came to see the Blind Traveller. What do you want with him you old gossip, the pappous said. If you've come to find him a wife, I hope you've got a better match than the one you made for my poor daughter.

I've come to see his face, Pourthitsa said. She was indignant with the pappous for insulting her match-making skills. Pourthitsa was a good matchmaker, so good that the villagers had never let her idiot son and her other four bastards starve.

She began matchmaking quite late in life. When she was still young a fisherman came to the village to fish eel. Back in his home town he said, he owned a huge fishmarket and smoked eel was a great delicacy there. Pourthitsa rode away on a cart full of eel. The fisherman blindfolded her so she would never find her way home again. Pourthitsa laughed at this. She had itchy feet, an adventurous heart, and she loved the taste of smoked eel. That's all the fisherman fed her till they reached his

home town.

Where this town was exactly she couldn't tell you. It took them years to get there and they travelled over mountains, across seas and she was blindfolded all the way. She stayed in this town for exactly one day. The fisherman, she said, was unspeakably cruel to her. If you asked her about the nature of this cruelty she would point very gently to her idiot son and then look down at the huge callouses on her feet. That's as far as you would get with Pourthitsa. But she did say that the village idiot was conceived amongst the black bream and the slippery sardines on that day, in a town where the chief characteristic of the people was their cruel and crooked smiles.

These are just the ravings of Pourthitsa, the villagers said. But Pourthitsa continued.

She had walked out of that cruel town in a feverish state, searching for kindness and someone to show her the way home. And she found it. A young gypsy took her to his carriage and bled the fever right out of her, face down on the wooden boards with thirty leeches on her back. She travelled with him from town to town bleeding the sick wherever they went until her idiot son was born. Then she became depressed.

Her first infidelity was with a fat balding man who owned a map of the world. Three nights she spent with him. They searched his map for her village but never found it. So she returned to her kind gypsy. She always did.

When she found her village it was twelve years later. She walked in with calloused feet, her four bastards clinging to her skirts and the idiot tied to her waist by a long rope. A rope which allowed him to stumble behind them with his withered leg and to dawdle the way idiots like to dawdle.

The Priest of Casia convinced her to untie her idiot son, whom she had tied to her ever since he could walk, and to work as his cook. In all truth she wasn't much of a cook and she was a terrible gossip as well. Ignorant woman, the Priest of Casia called her, but still he kept her on.

As for the kind gypsy, he went on his way and Pourthitsa did not think about him at all until her sons grew up. Then she searched their faces desperately for some resemblance to him and found none. On seeing the Blind Traveller, she said, they were right, he had a kind face. But she left yiayia Stella's house disappointed. That afternoon she sat on the priest's table (if you sit on the table they say you'll never marry) in a depressed mood, scaling two large fish.

It was on that same afternoon that Theodosios decided to send the sack of African banana chips to Vaia. With these he sent a young boy to tell his wife that things were not well in the village and she should take care.

They paid no attention whatsoever to the message,

and nibbled cautiously on the dried bananas wondering what they were. The pappous ate a little and spat it out.

Why, he's got cow shit for brains that son-in-law of ours.
Madness won't go to the mountain, the yiayia said.

The Blind Traveller chuckled and yiayia Stella inquired politely if perhaps you soaked them in water like beans. That night yiayia Stella cooked a borek—a little request which the Blind Traveller had made of Stella so that she had searched all over the village for exactly the right herbs. He had declared that it was simply delicious. It turned out that the Blind Traveller knew about everything, and he did not hesitate to give advice. When Vaia was baking bread he would call out to her.

Daughter is your bum sweating?
No pappous, it's not.
Well if your bum isn't sweating, daughter, then your bread's no good.

The Blind Traveller taught Vaia how to make good bread. The sort of bread that was later to make her bakery such a success.

The winter was coming. There was no doubt about it. The sparrows bathed in dirt and the swallows flew only a few feet off the ground. There was little food in

56

the village and even less money. Pappous Yiorgos noticed the sidelong glances the villagers gave him. One day the village women spat at Vaia by the well. As she drew water they gathered around her and spat at her face without saying anything. When she got home her veil was soaked in spit.

That week three things happened. On Monday Theodosios found an incredible olive tree, fully grown and already bearing fruit right in the middle of his field. On Tuesday a messenger came from the priest (acting on behalf of the village) demanding the ill-omened child be handed over to him. And on Friday the Blind Traveller regained his sight.

The Blind Traveller danced in the courtyard with no music and no light except for the moon and the stars. Theodosios sat down under the olive tree feeling very uneasy about things in general. Vaia veiled her face, wrapped her child in a wheat sack and went to see her husband.

Like a thief she entered his house. She woke him from his sleep with an embrace and then handed him his son. He dropped the child instantly, gave one scream and collapsed on the bed unconscious. Vaia slapped him around and poured water over his face.

When Theodosios came to, she thanked him for the fruit. But he could not keep his eyes off his son. Nor could he hide the look of disgust on his face. He said he had enjoyed sending her fruit. She said she had liked the white sweet chips the best. He said that they had cost him ten mats. They had come from Africa where they grew on trees. She threw herself at his feet and cried. He said he would get her more white chips if she wanted them. She said they were going to kill his son. He looked at the dreadful creature who was crawling about the room chasing after a cockroach. He became nauseous.

Oh, St. Vaia, we are lost, she sobbed.

He would speak to his father, Theodosios said. He would do what he could do.

Perhaps, Vaia said, taking his hand, perhaps he could save his son. Perhaps he could smuggle the child out to another town. After all, who would suspect him? Yes, there was a way.

Theodosios looked at the child sitting in the corner eating a cockroach. Some things are better left to fate, he said.

Vaia let go of his hand. She wiped her face with the edge of her veil and wrapped her child up. Before she walked out, Vaia told Theodosios that from this moment they were mortal enemies.

When the next day he sent her a bag of fresh bananas and dried figs she opened it and placed two centipedes, a scorpion, a handful of dead flies and a piece of mouldy cheese in the bag and sent it back.

When he was half-way back to Theodosios' house, yiayia Stella stopped Vaia's messenger and took the bananas out of the bag. She had never seen bananas. She thought that they were giant yellow okra. She thought that she would dry them and take their seeds. She would plant them and become famous for her giant okra, just like she had been for her tobacco plants. She went to hide the giant yellow okra in the shed and, to her surprise, she found the Blind Traveller (who was not blind any more) resting on a sack. No one had seen the Blind Traveller for several days. He told Stella that he had eaten them in Africa. He told her they were bananas and he showed yiayia Stella how to eat them. She laughed. She thought that bananas were funny. The two of them ate all the bananas, and yiayia Stella declared that bananas were better than bread.

THOUGH IT WAS MUCH TOO EARLY IN THE YEAR, PAPPOUS YIORGOS SLAUGHTERED THE

PIG Though it was much too early in the year, pappous Yiorgos slaughtered the pig and yiayia Stella concentrated all her skills to make the most delicious pork sausages. In those days yiayia Stella thought mostly of the Priest. For this story it would have been better if she had not thought of the Priest, if the Priest of Casia remained simply—the Priest. The Priest who had debated with the Blind Traveller. The Priest who had wanted to kill the gorilla child. But yiayia Stella thought of the Priest and of his mother, Silly Casia (with her lisp and frothy dribble), whose parents had kept her locked up for fifty years. Only when her bleeding days were over did they let her run free. From then on, every Sunday she would let out a white chicken and chase it down the street stark naked. Two young men who met on the square every Sunday morning called her theia Casia, and they would take her and the chicken home.

60

And just when her parents were going to die, in peace, having done their duty, Silly Casia slept with a travelling beggar and fell pregnant. The child who was born on Christmas day along with the spooks and the kallikandsarous was a remarkably beautiful child. It was such a shame people said, Silly Casia was hardly fit to bring up a child, and she was getting old. She was nearly sixty.

When Silly Casia's boy was ten and looking after this person and that person's goats for two pieces of bread and a bacon bone, the Old Abbot saw him. The Old Abbot was charmed by the boy's beauty. The Old Abbot wanted to take the boy away to live with him in the monastery. He would give the boy an education. The boy turned out to be remarkably clever. But Silly Casia said no. When they had taken him away, Silly Casia howled like a bitch, naked in the square, every day for two weeks. Then she stopped, and people said she had forgotten him.

Since Silly Casia was getting old, the Abbot placed her in the care of a large and very poor Turkish family. In return for this care, they would inherit her fields. Rumour had it that Mustapha hanged her in the shed with her own kerchief, just one year after her son had been taken. No one told him anything about it.

Fifteen years later they had brought the handsome young man's emaciated body home on the back of a wagon. Stella had peered over at the delirious man with his golden beard and full lips; she had thought it was Jesus himself. He did not want to be a priest. He wanted to leave. He wanted to leave the monastery. He would rather herd goats, he said. Yes, that is what he would rather do. As this was the time of the blood-pissing epidemic, no one paid much attention to his ravings.

Mirella nursed him back to health with her bitter herbs. Some people came to see him, but this was more out of curiosity than anything else. They came to see his beautiful feverish body which Mirella washed three times a day with St. Vaia's water and an old sea sponge. He did not like it in the monastery. Where was Casia, he wanted to know. Where was she? He wanted to know.

When he came out of the delirium, many young women would have married him. But he spent a week with Mirella and she spared him nothing. After that, he went back to the monastery.

Years later the Priest of Casia came back (he closed Mirella's house for a time, ruining her livelihood) and took up his position with a respectable paunch, a restrained smile and a passion for roasted pork sausages.

For her sausages, yiayia Stella used the best meat and just enough fat to ensure the sausages were not too greasy and not too dry. Pappous Yiorgos was sent to the town of Zandelli to bring back lemons and leeks.

He spent days travelling through towns searching for the right spices. The yiayia went to see the old ladies to get advice on the art of sausage making. But no one would let her into their house. Finally she veiled her face carefully and went to the Turkish quarters. The truth is that even though Allah forbade the Turks to eat pork, with their combination of spices they made the most delicious pork sausages. In the markets and bazaars these were sold as camel-meat delicacies. Yiayia Stella knocked on the doors, people peered through the shutters, saw it was the yiayia of the gorilla child, and then closed them again.

Finally Stella arrived at an old house where the windows and doors were nailed shut and it seemed to her a miracle that this house was still standing. She knocked at the door, and at first no one answered. Then there was movement in the house. Slowly the door opened, and standing before yiayia Stella was the foulest woman she had ever seen. The woman was tall but her back was bent at the waist so that yiayia Stella was looking down at the top of her head which had three wiry black hairs sticking out of it. The old woman twisted her neck back to see yiayia Stella. In the sunken eyes and toothless smile the yiayia saw Mirella the ancient whore. As a young girl Stella had heard stories about this house. Mirella had not been seen in the village for many years and people thought that she was dead. As for Mirella she looked carefully into Stella's face and saw that except for the grey hair and two wrinkles on her forehead Stella still seemed to have the face of her youth. The two women sat inside the parlour where the colours were mouldy and the fabrics were faded. For a good two hours they spoke about who were the living and who were the dead. Then yiayia Stella cleared her throat and thought it appropriate that she should begin talking about pork sausages. Mirella listened to yiayia Stella somewhat suspiciously at first. Yes, she knew exactly which herbs could make the most delicious sausages. But she must know what and whom they were for.

Here the yiayia had little choice but to tell the whole frightful story. Mirella did not seem at all disturbed by it, and in fact when yiayia Stella was telling her of the Blind Traveller she even closed her eyes and smiled to herself. When yiayia Stella had finished, Mirella spoke to her for hours on the art of making pork sausages. She explained what was the best way to clean the intestines without ruining them and what were the most useful herbs. Finally she told Vaia of a herb with a blue flower that grew in the damp behind St. Vaia's rock. Mirella refused the money Stella offered. She took the slabs of cheese and made yiayia Stella promise to come back in ten years time so they could again speak of who were the living and who were the dead.

Now, as it happened, just as the two women were speaking, the Elders were gathered in the Priest's house.

In one week they were planning to storm the house of pappous Yiorgos, break down the six-foot wall and, if necessary, kill the family. The monstrous child must be savaged by pigs, they said, as is the natural way of things. And if the weather permitted, a hog should be slaughtered so the people could sing and dance to the rising smell of pig's blood.

When pappous Yiorgos slaughtered his pig as early as October, the people of the village wondered what the Liaris household were up to. Some thought that this might even bring about snow. But it didn't. It brought sausages, and the weather was fine. When the sun came out they hung them on the balcony to dry. People whispered that they were sausages made of gorilla meat.

It was a Sunday. No one had actually set the exact date; people just knew that this was the date, and they gathered around the bridge waiting. There was an odd heat that day and Manolios the Kafedzis was serving cold water with three spoonsful of yoghurt. The clouds in the sky were red. The old yiayies said this was the blood of men killed in wars. Stefanos asked them about the wars. That week he moved all his things into the shed where Meta had once practised her boxing, and in his new room Stefanos began writing the histories of the village.

Vaia had known that they were coming. All week she had dreamed of fish. She woke up every morning feeling bitter. In the bath the night before, she had thought of drowning her child. But something had happened which she did not understand. And she knew it was too late for that.

The night before, yiayia Stella was overcome with sadness and she stole out of bed with the box of bones. All the time she was ashamed because she felt she was much too old for this sort of thing. She thought of Nestor and the first Vaia. She regretted having named her second daughter after such an unlucky child.

Very early that morning pappous Yiorgos had chained the gate shut. He waited outside with his two best dogs and his old gun. Yiayia Stella brought him in. It had taken a lot to convince her husband to come inside and unchain the gate. When she told him that what they were going to do was set up a stall by the side of the road and sell roast sausages to the crowd, he thought she had lost her mind. But she insisted on this.

The Priest of Casia and the men came down the cobbled street with their guns, angry dogs and squealing pigs. The three strongest men threw their bodies with all their strength against the gate, trying to knock it down.

Yiayia Stella came out and opened it. She made coffee for the men. Pappous Yiorgos explained that he had decided to feed the crowd with pork sausages, and asked would the men be good enough to help him set up a stall just by the bridge, and perhaps light a fire for him? Now this was hardly what they were expecting. The men were a little suspicious. They thought that pappous Yiorgos was going to poison the crowd. But the thought of roast pork sausages before Christmas made the Priest's mouth water.

As the men were setting up the stall, the crowd watched and whispered. The gorilla child was not going to be savaged by pigs but burnt on some sort of funeral pyre.

The crowd was uneasy.

Vaia came down the stairs perfectly composed. She handed her child to the Priest who held it away from his body as though it were diseased. He walked out of the gate like that, with the procession of men following him. When they could not possibly hear her, Vaia fell to the ground. She screamed and bashed her fists against the whitewash. The yiayia came out with the box of bones, placed them next to her weeping daughter, and hurried down the street to where her husband was preparing to cook the sausages.

People saw pappous Yiorgos hanging up the sausages and whispered that he had made the child into sausages. People yelled out obscenities at him, called him a cannibal, but no one dared get too close. The pappous calmly took the meat cleaver and began to cut the sausages into small pieces.

When the priest and his procession came with the

gorilla child, young women fainted, pregnant women miscarried, old yiayies crossed themselves, men buried their heads in their wife's breasts and moaned. Amidst the terror and confusion, yiayia Stella was cooking sausages and pappous Yiorgos was selling them.

Yiayia Stella's delicious pork sausages, four pieces for a drachma . . . fresh pork sausages with lemon and leek, four pieces for a drachma.

The Priest took the child to the bridge and prepared to release the pigs, but as soon as he turned around to give the order, the child crawled away. It began to crawl on the road to the town of Zandelli; people thought that the Priest should just let it crawl away. The Priest chased after it, picked it up and placed it on the foot of the bridge. But when he turned around again, the gorilla child crawled away. The Priest began talking to it angrily, entreating it to sit still. The child laughed and babbled back. The Priest ordered the men to tie it up. The men came and tied it up.

Just as the pigs were going to be released, the smell of the roast pork sausages hit the crowd. It was an extraordinary smell. People left the gorilla child and lined up at the stall. The Priest of Casia shook his fists in anger. He yelled at them to come back. They began to push and shove, afraid they might miss out; fights broke out. The smell spread to the village. Theodosios, the gorilla child's father, awoke from his drunken stupor and came to the bridge. Invalids began to scream in their beds till people came to get them. The yiayia and the pappous were run off their feet. When people ate their sausage they sat down by a tree or a rock, overcome with a warm feeling.

Yiayia Stella thought it odd that every time she went to the shed for another string of sausages, there was always one string still left. That is when she noticed that the Blind Traveller and all his things were gone. This continued till at last every man, woman and child of the village had eaten some of the most delicious pork sausage. When Vaia came out and untied her child and took him home, no one really cared. Yiayia Stella and pappous Yiorgos were exhausted, and when they packed up their stalls and went home they discovered that there was still one string of sausages left in the shed. They built a small fire in the courtyard and roasted it for lunch. As pappous Yiorgos ate the sausage, he thought how clever and remarkable his wife was to make such sausages. Vaia cut off tiny pieces of meat, chewed them in her mouth first, and then gave them to her son who ate them with obvious delight.

As yiayia Stella went to the well, she was struck by the stillness and quiet. Everyone had abandoned the sausage stall and some people were sleeping on the streets. The streets were full of still bodies and white sausage wrappers. When the wind came, the wrappers flew about like a swarm of angry insects. The village was dreaming. If you had walked down the streets, or even entered the people's houses—which you could very well have done since the people in this village never locked their doors—you would have seen their eyelids fluttering like butterflies. They were smiling curiously, as if what they were seeing was pleasurable despite the fact that it was somewhat puzzling. The yiayia filled her bucket and thought no more of the stillness. Now if pappous Yiorgos had known of Mirella's flowers, he would have been on his knees praying to the saints.

For in those days Mirella was known for her powerful potions. Some of her dried powder in an urn of sand can curse your family for generations. A bitter herb in your bean stew can kill. And a drop of her potion in your coffee can drive you into a passion to make your head spin. This passion might last a few days, months, even years. But, as it is impossible to tell precisely when it ends, you might be left spinning for a lifetime.

There was Socrates who got drunk and chased Ritsa around the village with an axe till he was exhausted. Even after six children she was a good runner. When Socrates lost sight of her, he would just sit down and cry. She was a terrible cook, slow and cumbersome on the fields, she nagged continuously, she still couldn't produce one male heir, and above all she had no neck.

70

It was as if, he thought, God had hammered her head straight on to her shoulders.

After they had lain together in her father's fields (this was when he was young and hopeful) he had not thought of her again till he heard that she had swallowed half a bottle of bleach. Everyone was saying that Ritsa had lain with Socrates. Everyone was saying that he had tricked her, that he would never marry her. And she drank half a bottle of bleach to wash away the shame. When he had heard about this, he had laughed at her. But after that one coffee she gave him, he could not bear to be away from her. When she was not around him, when he could not see her, he felt sick. Every night he slept under her window. In the morning her mother shook the tablecloth on him and filled his eyes with bread crumbs. He paid Pourthitsa the Matchmaker dearly with eggs and corn, but straight after the marriage the effect of that coffee wore off and he began to look wistfully at the necks of other men's wives. It was said that Mirella's potions could ruin lives.

Then there were the neighbours who had feuded for years. How it had begun no one remembered, not even them. They never came to blows. It was just hate. With hate, one neighbour could will his neighbour's field of blossoming almond trees cut down while simply eating his evening meal. With hate, one could make another's animals fall ill while just sitting on the toilet. In church if one neighbour concentrated enough he could make his neighbour's haemorrhoids burst and bloody his white Sunday breeches. Their hate was so great that, when a minor tremor went through the village, their houses were the only ones to fall. When the blood-pissing epidemic struck, they both concentrated their hatred on each other with such precision that it cancelled itself out. Everyone around them was dying and they were the healthiest men in the village.

When they were old pappouthes, having married off their children, their only wish was to live to see their neighbour die first. Every time the dogs howled in the night and the church bells rang, they would send their wives out to check who had died. When the first neighbour's wife died, the second neighbour knew that he was going to win. Deaf to the protests of his children, he sold all his fields and threw a celebration for the village. There were six pigs roasting on the spit, huge pots with goat stew, and pickled red capsicums stuffed with cabbage and carrot. He paid for a whole troop of northern gypsies. There were dancing girls, dancing monkeys and even dancing bears. There were fortune-tellers from China and whores from Cairo. There was honey for the children, coloured ribbons for their hair. This feast went on for a week.

The first neighbour closed himself up in his house. But even in his sleep he heard the rhythmic beat of the daouli and he dreamt always of the coloured skirts of gypsy women. When after a week no one saw or heard

72

anything from the first neighbour, the second neighbour assumed he had died of grief or was probably on his deathbed. So the second neighbour sold his house to keep the festivities going for yet another week.

After two weeks the celebrations ended and everyone went home. Except for the second neighbour who did not have a home to go to. (His wife and children had spurned him for wasting all their money in the feasting.) Just when he had made up his mind to sleep out in the town square, the first neighbour, much to everyone's surprise, hobbled out and invited his neighbour round for that fateful plate of bean stew.

After all these years what they finally spoke about no one knows. Perhaps they spoke of their hatred and tried to trace its roots. Or perhaps their conversation was polite and civilised, something like this.

Fuck my mother, this is a damned good stew neighbour.
Yes, the only thing, bless her soul, Martha taught me to make.

Or perhaps the two neighbours just sat opposite each other eating their bean stew, slurping, spitting and wiping their plates clean with a chunky piece of bread. After dinner they drank half a bottle of raki, and the first neighbour rolled cigarettes which they smoked and passed between them, all the time not saying one single word. Well after midnight when the plate was full of cigarette butts, the second neighbour got up to leave. The first neighbour saw him to the door. And at the gate the second neighbour turned around and said.

What's been said here tonight, neighbour, let's just keep it between the two of us.

And with that he turned around and disappeared into the night.

What was really said that night no one will ever know. What is known is that both neighbours died on that night and the dogs howled and the bells rang for both of them at precisely the same time. The villagers said that Mirella's herbs could kill.

Then there is the house of the Karasakathes—forever barren, just like a desert. You might go there even today, clean out the oven, light the fire and roast yourself some pork. If it's a sunny day, you may decide to enjoy your food outside in the courtyard. But when you are about half-way through your meal the sand and grit between your teeth will make you stop. In the end you will not be able to taste the meat from the sand. In disgust you will throw your meat down on the ground. It will not be the flies or the ants or even the birds that get the meat, but the sand. A warm wind will blow, and you will watch the meat get covered by sand till it disappears. And you will rush out of the house in a despairing mood. So, perhaps if you're in the area you should avoid visiting the house of the Karasakathes, or at least avoid wasting a good meal there.

Now the Karasakathes were once the richest family in the village, with many fields, a daughter and a son. But their good fortune was matiased because their daughter was ruined somewhere around the age of seven. People said she ruined herself while riding a horse. The midwife never checked, but everyone knew she was ruined. Her family just came to accept it. But the father could not, and behind his wife's back he kept offering fields to find his daughter a husband. But no one would marry a ruined Karasakathina.

When the girl reached puberty her mother brought her to the brothel. The mother did not take money. She only asked that Mirella give the girl a different name and not allow her to return home. Mirella guessed what no one else had, and on the first night broke the girl's hymen with two fingers greased in pork fat. The girl was very popular and brought much money in to the house.

The family disowned that daughter and went on with their lives. The son brought a wife from the city, a beautiful young woman who took over the running of the household so that the mother could rest in her old age. The father began to lose his eyesight, but he could not keep his mind off his young daughter. He began frequenting the brothel, just to catch a glimpse of her or to hear how she was getting on. When he found out that the other whores hated her he felt afraid for her. The old man came to the brothel and gave Mirella money so that she would look after his daughter.

When the old man caught the disease, his daughter-in-law said he was a stupid old man, spending all his money at the whorehouse. What about her five children? At this rate there would be nothing left for them. She sent him to the hospital in the city to be cured. When he came back, he could hardly see at all but he insisted on helping his daughter-in-law about the house. The daughter-in-law was pleased with his industry—he would do all the heavy work, like bringing the water from the well. But the father would actually fill the urns the night before with lentils or salt. In the morning he would come to the brothel, empty the urns out in Mirella's store house, get news of his daughter, and return home with his urns filled with water. When she found out his scheme, the daughter-in-law was furious. One night she emptied out the lentils and filled the urns with sand. In the morning the old man who was almost blind came to the brothel with his urns filled with sand.

Sand won't buy you kindness old man, Mirella said.

The old man returned home with the urns. He took handfuls of sand and threw it in the courtyard and at the house. All the time he was cursing.

76

Sand! Now you'll see sand. Where I sow sand, a desert will grow. Where I sow sand, a desert will grow!

He smashed the urns and left a mess in the courtyard. which the daughter-in-law and the mother had always kept so clean. After that, the old man never went to see his daughter in the brothel again.

The daughter-in-law nursed her father-in-law with great care until the day he died. She said the disease had affected his brain, and she kept him in bed all day. She fed him on lemon rice for the rest of his life. But as hard as she tried, the daughter-in-law could never manage to clean up all the sand. Sand was always getting in their hair, their eyes and even in their food. The blood-pissing epidemic came and took all her five children. The daughter-in-law became a nervous fidgety woman. The son locked the house and took his wife and mother to live in the city. The villagers said that Mirella's powders could ruin families for generations.

There was no need for the pappous to tell his wife about the dangers of Mirella's flowers. The yiayia knew all this. In fact, as the wind rose, the white sausage wrappers danced and she was reminded of the second neighbour's celebration. She did not wash the dishes; she just lay next to her husband and dreamed. She dreamed of wild things. Mirella's potions can make you dream of wild things.

TWO

IN PRISON META IS KEPT IN A DARK ROOM

In prison Meta is kept in a dark room and raped. She is raped by the person who brings her water. The warden rapes her, the visitors rape her, the gardener rapes her. Even the cousin of the man who lives across the road, and comes to the town every summer with his consumptive daughter—he rapes her.

One day Meta turns into a man. No one knows who he is. There is no name and no record of his crime. So he is set free.

Meta works as a blind shoe-polisher on the street corner just across the road. Being blind gives him an advantage over the shoe-polisher who works on the square. He even does better than the begging gypsy mother with her maimed twins.

It is not a bad existence. Bitter cold in the winter but the summer is pleasant. And Eleni, the consumptive daughter of the cousin of the man who owns the house across the road, always comes to town in the summer. With her pale face, her wretched cough and a handkerchief bloodied with phlegm held to her mouth.

On Sunday evenings Meta and Eleni sit on the broken curb eating apricots and peaches from Eleni's uncle's farm. When she knows her house is empty, Eleni takes Meta there. She helps him climb up to the roof, and the two of them sit there. The mountain breeze blows across their faces. Eleni comes here for this. The doctors say it's good for her lung. She pulls Meta's hand into her blouse and runs his fingers round and round her belly and up and down a scar that runs across her chest. She has only one lung now. They threw the other one out in Paris when it filled with pus. People see them on the roof smoking, laughing and stroking each other's bellies.

Next summer Eleni does not come to the town. Eleni never comes to the town again.

Meta is seized with anxious feelings that he never knew as a woman. He wanders about the world searching for Eleni. He herds goats in Albania. He becomes a Jewish dentist in Paris. He marries again, has children. He loses everything in the war. He escapes to Africa as a male whore.

Behind a sleazy Egyptian bar he hears the story of his gorilla grandchild. That's when he wanders back into the village as a Blind Traveller.

ON THE DAY THAT META FACES STEFANOS

*On the day that Meta faces Stefanos she wears silk underwear
and a stylish red dress. Her feet are in little gold sandals
which match the gold belt around her waist. Hanging off this
belt is a sheath, and in this sheath is a dagger.*

*Kostas the Butcher is mesmerised by her feet, the dainty
toes that peek out of the golden sandals. The pappous cannot
keep his eyes off the twitching muscles of her shoulders. The
yiayia has eyes only for the curve of her waist, and Vaia, for
the dagger that hangs from it.*

*Meta finds Stefanos in the fields with his son. The first
thing Theodosios sees is her nipples pointing out from beneath
her red dress. Theodosios never recognises his mother. He is
still waiting for the goat with fourteen nipples. Meta smooths
her hair back and speaks with her son about fertilisers.*

*Then she draws her dagger and goes to face Stefanos. He
is on his haunches, under the olive tree scratching the earth
and searching, he explains, for ancient things. She bends
down, collects a handful of dirt and eats it, rocks and all.*

83

She rips a branch off the olive tree and eats it. She climbs up the tree, takes her silk underwear off and shits on her husband's head: hard shit with little rocks and pips in it. Stefanos wipes the shit from his head and continues to scratch the earth.

Before she leaves, Meta gives Stefanos the dagger so that he can dig the earth without ruining his fingers. He smiles up at her, a sweet toothless smile.

Some people say it is not Meta that has returned but an impostor who has stolen her name and her desire. They say the real Meta would have stabbed Stefanos straight through the heart.

Meta leaves the field and never sees her husband again until the day he walks into the village with dried brain on his shirt and a shard of bone sticking out of the wound that was once his left eye.

BEFORE META COMES TO ME SHE SITS IN THE KAFENEIO DRINKING RAKI

Before Meta comes to me she sits in the kafeneio drinking raki. Out of her pocket she takes a box and places it on the table with a loud thump. She opens the box and in it is a set of flashing white teeth. She leans back in her chair and smiles. She looks around the room and her gaze stops on Meriklis the Grave-digger. In the silence pappous Meriklis' knees begin to knock together. He protests in terrified groans. He looks around the kafeneio for his son who is hiding under the table. Meta sits Meriklis next to her and buys him drinks. When he is drunk, she leans over and pulls out his two remaining teeth. She gets him to throw his head back and fits him with a set of gleaming white teeth. Meriklis the Grave-digger smiles with what the villagers say is the smile of a murdered man. But Meriklis the Grave-digger loves his new teeth, and he just keeps on smiling like a silly casia. After Meta leaves, Meriklis the Grave-digger buys drinks for everyone. When the news reaches his house, his wife, yiayia Meriklis, runs to the kafeneio to see if it is true. She begs her husband to throw these teeth out so that the dead man's soul will not come for them. But Meriklis the Grave-digger is in love with his new smile and besides, he says, he is from a family accustomed to dead men's things.

Meta comes to me fierce and desirable, with a set of white teeth wrapped in red silk. She paints the brothel blue. She fills the balcony with pots of purple flowers and plants a vegetable garden at the back. She brings a pig, two goats and a dozen chickens. In the winter she rubs oil into my back. In the summer we sit on the verandah knitting. In the spring we fit teeth. In one room I pull out teeth and prepare people's gums. In the other room Meta gives people new smiles. The young people say, Meta who carries that ancient whore to bed every night, is filling the village with murdered men's smiles. But the old people pay good money to eat meat again and to smile again. In the autumn I lie in bed, too happy to sleep, and not even one dead man comes to reclaim his smile. That's how generous the dead are.

IT IS STARVING BEBA THE TURKISH WIDOW
WHO BRINGS THE CHILD TO US   *It is Starving*
*Beba the Turkish widow who brings the child to us when she
leaves the village to marry a widower with two sons. Afraid
of what her stepsons may do to her daughter, she leaves her
with us. Meta is so delighted with the child, she calls her
Agape.*

*The first night Agape cries and cries for Starving Beba.
Meta collects her tears in a porcelain vase. I bathe her with
warm water and perfumed oils. Together we paint the ceiling
of Agape's room with giant yellow flowers, so that every night
Agape will sleep under a field of giant chamomile.*

*I teach Agape how to read the future in chicken entrails,
and how to make poisons to kill off her enemies. Meta takes
her hunting through the Valley of Blood. She teaches Agape
how to immobilise a wild boar with one fierce look. But in
these days of running though the mountain Agape never sees
a wild boar, not even one. I suppose this is just as well, for
she is much too happy for her ferocity to appear sincere. And*

Meta says that a wild boar can pick an impostor from a mile away. When Agape sleeps, Meta and I watch over her, and we synchronise our breathing with hers.

Agape becomes so beautiful that Meta cannot watch over her any more without crying. Agape has her first bleeding. She takes off her underpants and passes them round the tables of the kafeneio. I teach her to read and she reads everything. At home she reads the books from my mother's boxes, and she reads the chicken entrails while Meta prepares our dinner.

One night six suitors come to sing outside the blue house. Meta wakes up and runs to Agape's room. And on this dark and moonless night the room is lit up by Agape's face. I plant bushes of stinging nettles outside Agape's window. Meta veils Agape's face and keeps her indoors.

One night the suitors quarrel over her and knock each other out with rocks. Agape of the Glowing Face yawns with relief and says that at last she will get some sleep. The Priest of Casia, that old goatbeard, comes to the blue house. Mirella, he says, that girl of yours must marry. With a sharpened knife Meta waits for the husband to come. But despite the singing suitors no husband comes.

One day the Pale Millionaire comes to the village with a league of good men to drain the swamp, with promises of food and fields for everyone. His men dig here, they sink their rods there, and the Pale Millionaire stands by like a captain. In his right hand he holds a bag of money and in his left a wooden cane with beautifully carved designs. He is so sophisticated that the village girls make love to him with their eyes.

They follow him about and swoon at his feet. Without turning his head, he tosses them a coin or two. On Sundays people take their families to the marshland with a hamper of tomatoes, boiled eggs and fresh bread so they can eat and watch the workers and laugh.

When he hears about Agape of the Glowing Face, the Pale Millionaire goes straight to the blue house. His plan is to take her to Athens and put her on his balcony so everyone in the district will see that the Pale Millionaire has a bright young wife with a face that shines like the moon. Meta wants to impale him with his own cane. Agape agrees to marry him but insists that she will never leave the blue house.

A week before the wedding I break Agape's hymen with two fingers greased in pig fat. The morning after the wedding night, Meta hangs the bride's sheets in the town square for all to see. All day the villagers laugh at the sheets with no virgin stain. In the night, they hung the horns of the biggest goat on the door of the house where Agape and the Pale Millionaire sleep. Whenever they see the Pale Millionaire in the kafeneio, where he buys drinks for everyone, the villagers snicker and make the sign of the horns. One day he gets so angry that he swings at someone with his cane and breaks it. Meta laughs all night. But Agape is grateful that she can unveil her glowing face again and run through the streets. In the kafeneio she tells everyone who will listen what it is like making love with the Pale Millionaire under a field of chamomile. She boasts of a pleasure which at its peak turns her glowing face into a flash of light. At this point, she says, her husband always closes his eyes.

After just one year of this, the humiliated husband walks out of the village leaving only his broken cane and acres of muddy fields. Where the marshland was, there are fields, and children run across them filling their buckets with muddy eel and fish. Up in the mountain it snows and a freezing wind blows across the village. At night fishermen gather in the square with torches, threatening to sow the new fields with salt, while outside the house of her young lover a woman slowly turns to ice. Agape goes to the kafeneio to find the broken cane because, she says, that's all that her husband left her. That's when she begins selling her sexual favours to travelling tinkers and tobacco merchants. Not because she misses her husband or needs the money but because it keeps away the suitors. That is how the brothel begins again. The days of fitting teeth and knitting in the sun are over.

THREE

**YIORGOS THE APEFACE WOKE UP EVERY
MORNING WITH A COLD AND BLEARY LIGHT
IN HIS EYES** Yiorgos the Apeface woke up every
morning with a cold and bleary light in his eyes and
the smell of fresh bread. He filled his baskets with
twenty-two loaves and rode across the village. Yiorgos
the Apeface was a polite man, of a basically lonesome
nature. He lived a quiet life and was betrothed to a girl
from a distant town. He spent his mornings delivering
bread for his mother's bakery and his afternoons cutting
wood. In this ordinary life there was one thing that
Yiorgos the Apeface liked especially to do. That was to
sit in a corner of the shed when all the work was over
and read.

But whenever his mother, who grew up well before
the first school began, found a book, she used it to light
the fire. Vaia found her son's reading irritating. Yiorgos
the Apeface was not a child any more, nor was he a
schoolmaster. Reading could only encourage his lone-

some nature. So when he finished his work, Vaia found more work for him to do. If he finished this work she sent him to help old Manolios the Kafedzis.

When Manolios the Kafedzis died, leaving no children of his own, Yiorgos the Apeface naturally took over the kafeneio. Now, being such a famed miser, people wondered what had happened to Manolios' money. During the night they kept digging up his grave to see if he had not taken it with him. In the end Meriklis the Grave-digger took the body out of the graveyard and buried it somewhere in an empty field. When the League of Good Men called this an unholy burial, Meriklis the Grave-digger said Manolios was not a holy man. He was the sort of man who would have liked the idea of being buried in an unmarked grave. As for his money, the truth is he had most probably spent it. For in his last days he had fallen on hard times. In the Days of Progress the kafeneio was just a place for old men to play with their worry beads.

In the Days of Progress people worked like ants. There was a school, a doctor, a League of Good Men and never enough food. The League of Good Men drained the marsh and made new fields. Most of the villagers worked on the fields of the marshland and were paid by the League of Good Men in yellow slips. In the village these slips came to replace legal tender. The villagers could buy what they needed with the yellow slips in the League of Good Men's store. And it

94

was on one of these days that the gorilla child was christened Yiorgos of the Apeface. How hairy was Yiorgos the Apeface? To his betrothed (descriptions to a betrothed are bound to be flattering) he had been described as hairy, in a manly, handsome sort of way.

Yiorgos the Apeface was an industrious man. He spent all week cleaning the kafeneio, scrubbing the floorboards, painting the walls and repairing broken chairs. He no longer had time to read and for this Vaia was relieved. On Sundays he put on his best suit, brushed his hair neatly, and waited patiently for the people to come. A few old men came, drank Turkish coffee, and played with their worry beads. Shy as Yiorgos the Apeface was, he came to enjoy the company of these old men.

Now one day, among the many fine things that the League of Good Men brought to the store, were buckets of octopus. But the people of the village did not like the look of them. Even after the Doctor declared that octopus could cure headaches, backaches, make your daughter's breasts grow round and her cheeks glow rosy, people still did not buy them. The League of Good Men squabbled about who ordered the octopus. And when they saw that the octopus would be thrown out, the League of Good Men declared they would give it to the kafeneio of Yiorgos the Apeface.

Theodosios, who was a foreman in the League of Good Men's fields, was sent to the house of Vaia and

Yiorgos the Apeface with two buckets of octopus. Theodosios had not been to his wife's house for many years
on account of them being mortal enemies. (But in the
brothel it was well known to the whores that he cried
out his wife's name in his sleep.) Theodosios left the
octopus in the courtyard. When she recognised him,
Vaia chased her husband out of the house with a loaf
of hot bread. But Yiorgos the Apeface accepted the
buckets of octopus because it was the only thing his
father had ever given him. Secretly he was delighted by
it.

Not knowing what to do with all this octopus,
Yiorgos the Apeface went to the store and bought red
wine and sacks of onions. That week people walked
past the kafeneio and saw him beating the octopus on
the verandah. In the Days of Progress this was an odd
sight indeed, and people dawdled outside just so they
could watch. Yiorgos the Apeface pounded the octopus
until it was tender and cooked it in the wine. He also
collected wild cherries and made a wild cherry drink.
He painted a sign on a board, a modest sign with little
black letters. Those who could not read asked their
children what it said. It said simply that there was a
wild cherry drink to be bought in the kafeneio for five
drachmas. That Sunday many people wandered into the
kafeneio just to have a look.

No one was more surprised than Yiorgos the Apeface
himself. And, being such a shy man, he became

instantly afraid. He thought the people might become drunk, break windows and start a riot. But this did not happen. The people were very well behaved. They sat in the kafeneio and spoke to each other softly and sensibly. Women minded their children so they did not run about the place but sat quietly at their parents' feet. Men were especially polite to their wives. Of course everyone asked about the wild cherry drink, and those who had five drachmas even got to taste it. As for the tender octopus in wine sauce, everyone daring enough to try it agreed on what a fine meal it was. That night no one stayed too late or laughed too loud. The League of Good Men, who were sleeping only streets away, had no idea of what was happening in the kafeneio of Yiorgos the Apeface.

From then on the kafeneio of Yiorgos the Apeface was open every night. The people looked forward to it all day. Yiorgos the Apeface mostly stood behind the bar. He was still a shy man, still with a lonesome nature, but it appeared that he was cured at least of his reading habit.

When the League of Good Men heard about the gatherings they went to the kafeneio of Yiorgos the Apeface to put an end to all the mischief. But when they got there they had to admit that there was no mischief, that everyone was well behaved. Everyone was laughing, but there appeared to be no drunkards. The meals were delicious and well priced. The wild

97

cherry drink that everyone wanted was a sweet children's drink with no spirits at all. Before they left they demanded that Yiorgos the Apeface at least pay for the octopus they had given him. In this payment, Yiorgos the Apeface was prompt.

As people got used to each other, the kafeneio of Yiorgos the Apeface became a very lively sort of place. Yiorgos the Apeface did something quite uncharacteristic of himself. He bought a gaitha from a travelling tinker and taught himself to play it. When everyone was seated and served, he sat on the end of the bar and played his gaitha, and the people said that he had quite an ear for music.

There was almost no one in the village who did not make an appearance at the kafeneio. Vaia put on her one good dress and came to her son's kafeneio. She went from table to table serving food. Theodosios saw her there one night and wondered at how lovely she had become. It was at the kafeneio that you found out who was born and who had died, who was paying what for the crop, who was in love and who was not. It was there that Abdul brought Fatime for a glass of cold water while she waited for the bus to take her to the town where she went for her countless abortions. It was there that the villagers first heard how Old Koulousios was sleeping with Young Koulousios' wife. Sunday was a particularly good night because there were strangers from other towns, with news of the world.

Now, the wild cherry drink never went up in price. As the modest sign said, it was five drachmas a glass. But the problem was that the wild cherry drink could only be bought with drachmas, and most of the villagers, who worked in the League of Good Men's fields, had little money, only the League of Good Men's yellow slips. Of course there were meals, tasty mezethes and many other drinks to be bought with the League of Good Men's yellow slips, but the wild cherry drink, as the modest sign said, cost five drachmas.

For those with money the wild cherry drink was popular. The League of Good Men bought bottles of it to help put their children to sleep. Other men said that they wanted to buy some for their children too. Kostas the Butcher, who could not bear to miss out on anything, bought four whole bottles with money his wife had been saving for months. His daughter Marianthe came to cry in the kafeneio because that money had been to buy her green velvet from the travelling merchant. She had red hair and the man she loved would only have her in green velvet.

The League of Good Men made up a cherry drink of their own and sold it in the store for only one slip. But no one bothered to buy the wild cherry drink of the League of Good Men. In his rooms the Doctor told all the people that if they drank the wild cherry drink of the kafeneio, worms would grow in their mouths and eat their teeth, but no one paid any attention to the Doctor.

In the fields of the marshland Theodosios made a tired speech about how long and hard life seemed. He said the marsh had once belonged to everyone. He said now they were breaking their backs all day in these lands while the League of Good Men just sat on their arses. Theodosios took a handful of the League of Good Men's yellow slips from his pocket and set fire to them. The other men threw their yellow slips on the fire too. In the eyes of the field workers, Theodosios' face had dignity. They left the fields vowing never to return.

The League of Good Men brought in others to work their fields. They came to the village in forty carriages. The strangest collection of field workers the villagers had ever seen. They were made up mostly of mercenary soldiers and beggars with shifty eyes. There was also a tribe of women. Beautiful dark women who belonged to no one but themselves, proud women with faint moustaches. There was even a famous one-legged cut-throat (just released from prison) who kept tobacco and alcohol in his wooden leg. They pitched their tents near the fields and sat around fires singing songs that sounded to the villagers like barbaric war cries. Within two days there was not even one lock left in the League of Good Men's store.

In the night a band of masked thieves emptied out the store of the League of Good Men. People said it was the foreigners and they wanted to go down and throw them out of the village. The League of Good Men said it was Theodosios and his workers. They said those lazy thieves would go to prison. Theodosios and his workers fled to the mountains but the thieving continued. People set fire to the houses of Theodosios' workers for causing all this trouble. Others blamed the League of Good Men for bringing foreigners into the village. Whenever they could, they secretly sent food to the mountain for Theodosios and his men. Many young men, sons of workers, left their homes and went to the mountain to join Theodosios.

After dark, people locked themselves inside. If they had to go outside they always travelled in groups. They said that the cutthroat with his wooden leg lurked in dark places. He snuck upon you so silently that you were gone before you knew it.

These are strange times, Meriklis the Grave-digger was heard whispering in the kafeneio. He was walking along a dirt track one day when three men jumped out of the bush, threw him to the ground and tied him up. One of the men, who was wearing a mask, kicked and punched Meriklis in the stomach before dragging him by the ear into his own backyard and pointing to a cluster of plants the man said were poisonous. He said Theodosios was going to use them to poison the water supply. Poison, Meriklis said he knew nothing of poison, he thought the plants were parsley. The masked men punched him in the stomach again, uprooted his plants and fled. Strange times indeed.

The League of Good Men took the families of fourteen of the lazy thieves out of the village to relatives in other towns who could protect them until their loony husbands came down from the mountain. Many were crying because they did not want to go. They took wives and daughters, children, yiayies and pappouthes. All in all they took fifty-seven people, among them the father of Theodosios. Stefanos did not want to go with them. He protested that he had no relatives outside the village, but one of the mercenaries took him by the hand and broke his wrist.

Pappous Yiorgos hid his wife and daughter. Together with Yiorgos the Apeface they poured buckets of water over their house and soaked all their things. But no one came to set their house on fire or take anyone away.

Despite everything, on Sunday the kafeneio of Yiorgos the Apeface continued. But the kafeneio had changed in character. The air was thick with smoke and the smell of hate and fear. The foreigners came to get drunk. The beautiful dark women who belonged to no one but themselves came to dance with each other and sometimes, people said, fucked the spies of the League of Good Men behind the counter. Those who supported Theodosios came, and those who did not, came. Fights broke out but remarkably no one was ever killed there. Even Theodosios and his band of men, who were out-

102

lawed in this village, came to boast of their conquests. If the League of Good Men wanted to catch Theodosios in the kafeneio of Yiorgos the Apeface it would have been easy. But they never came to the kafeneio. No one could understand why.

People thought it was Theodosios that the League of Good Men feared. For in the village the myth of Theodosios was growing. This happened over one night in particular. Theodosios got word of the League of Good Men's visit to the brothel. That night the women and children of the League of Good Men were to be at the loom weaving by lamplight.

Theodosios and his men came down to rob one of the Good Men's houses but the wife of that house had left her sleeping baby behind. And in the middle of the night it woke up screaming. The men ignored it and went on with their thieving. But then its cries grew louder and all the brave men of Theodosios, who had left their houses to come to the mountains, began to sweat.

Throw it in the fire, Theodosios said.

One of the brave young men went in the room, got the baby, and threw it in the fire. The room lit up like a carnival and at that moment the myth of Theodosios grew huge.

As Theodosios and his men were escaping they were attacked by the mercenaries who were supposed to have been guarding the house but had only just returned from a drinking party. The brave young man who had thrown the baby in the fire was shot. Theodosios and his men dragged his body back to the mountain. But because they were being chased and he was slowing them down, they buried him in a shallow grave just outside the house of Meriklis the Grave-digger.

In the morning the dogs dug up the body and Meriklis found it. He cleaned it up and took it to the square for the boy's family to collect. The boy's mother came to the square where she threw herself onto the body and howled. Everyone in the village stopped what they were doing and listened to that howling. Yiayia Stella pushed her face up against the gate and for a moment she closed her eyes.

When it was very dark Vaia went to the mountain. She took a stick and she beat Theodosios on the head for causing so much trouble. Out of respect, the men of Theodosios left the camp while his wife was beating him.

Out of the fifty-seven taken from the village Stefanos was the only one to return. Stella, who was standing at the gate, was the first one to see him. There was dried brain all over his shirt and a shard of bone sticking out of the wound which had once been his left eye. Your father-in-law has been sleeping with the dead, Stella said. Vaia noticed that wherever Stefanos walked fat flies followed him so they could lay their maggots on

104

him. Stella sent her daughter to the brothel to ask Meta and Mirella what they should do with him. After midnight Agape of The Glowing Face was sent down. She covered Stefanos with a cloak and took him to the brothel where he hid for many days. After attending to his wounds Mirella washed him with perfumed oils. But his smell did not go away. The whores and their clients complained about it. Meta moved him to a tiny back room. However Agape seemed not to mind his smell at all for she went to see him every day. Because of his broken wrist he dictated the rest of his histories to her.

Now the spies of the League of Good Men, the enemies of Theodosios, were everywhere. A rumour spread through the village that Stefanos had returned and was hiding in the brothel. The whores became afraid that their house would be burnt down. To fight this rumour Meta began to spread a rumour of her own. The rumour said that on Sunday Stefanos would appear at the kafeneio of Yiorgos the Apeface. In these times when everyone watched their words carefully, the rumour of Stefanos' return spread quickly. Some were denying it, others were predicting that terrible things would come of it.

On that Sunday people came to the kafeneio in droves. Meta combed her hair, put on her grey striped breeches and a clean bandage on her husband's eye. But Stefanos refused to go. Meta told him that in the crowd he would be safe. She said that if everyone saw that he was alive no one would dare touch him. But Stefanos was still afraid to go. Meta went to the courtyard and got the gun. She said it would be better for her to do this. Stefanos got up but fell down again. He said his feet would not carry him. So Meta lifted him up, threaded her arm through his and held his hand. They walked to the kafeneio holding onto each other like young lovers. In the kafeneio she sat next to him. But there was no need for Meta to guard Stefanos, for his smell alone kept people away.

When they arrived Yiorgos the Apeface announced that for this night the wild cherry drink was free. Theodosios brought out a box of dried chillies, to kill the worms that eat your teeth, he said. Yiorgos the Apeface passed them around the kafeneio, he was so delighted with the second thing his father ever gave him. Vaia did not chase Theodosios away, though she wanted to. People drank wild cherry drink to their heart's delight. That night Yiorgos the Apeface did something so uncharacteristic of himself that people fell out of their chairs. He sang a song. He sang a funny song telling the story of the League of Good Men and the wild cherry drink. They laughed so loud the League of Good Men could not sleep.

The next day vicious rumours swept the village. But certainly the most vicious of all the rumours was one which could be traced back to the League of Good Men.   **106**

It said that Yiorgos the Apeface was not a man like ordinary men. Yiorgos the Apeface, they said, was an animal. On the way to work people went past the kafeneio so they could look at him. Even those who were sceptical about such rumours peered into the kafeneio to see the hairy kafedzis. At first they were relieved to see Yiorgos the Apeface wiping down the bar, looking as he had always looked. But, as they went off to work, they felt somehow uneasy about him.

When the news reached his house, Yiorgos the Apeface went to see himself in the mirror but he could not see anything he had not seen before. How ugly was he? Well, one story said that when he was five (and still without a name, and too heavy to be baptised in a church) yiayia Stella and Meta took him to the marsh. Meta dipped him in the water and pulled him out again. The yiayia christened him Yiorgos of the Apeface because she believed in calling a thing by its name.

Yiayia Stella became afraid that the news would somehow reach his betrothed and she would never come for her husband. Rumours spread that the betrothed was a girl with unusually large ears. People said they had seen her with their own eyes. So large, people said, that they flapped about like elephant's ears. People became afraid that a girl with such remarkably large ears might have remarkable hearing—she might be able to hear what went on behind walls and closed doors.

The Doctor said that they should send Yiorgos the Apeface to be cured in Paris. The League of Good men agreed that Yiorgos the Apeface should go to Paris, only the Doctors from Paris could cure the poor man. But the Doctors from Paris did not come to the village and neither did the betrothed.

Despite everything, the kafeneio of Yiorgos the Apeface continued more popular than ever. Yiorgos the Apeface continued to sing his funny songs, and people came to hear him. The funny songs that Yiorgos the Apeface sang were about people in the village. Sometimes people recognised themselves in a song and swore that they would never put foot in this shit-hole again. They missed one week, maybe two, but sure enough by the next week they would sneak in very late and sit at the back with a sour expression. People said he was a funny gypsy, a spiteful freak, a real character, a Turk. But the truth was, that when all was said and done he was just a good kafedzis.

At about this time Stefanos finished dictating his histories to Agape. That night he came to Stella's house, picked up his grandson in a carriage and took him out of the village. They rode together for many hours until they reached a clearing from which came a terrible stench. There Stefanos stopped his carriage and Yiorgos the Apeface began to gag. It was a dark moonless night, so dark that they could barely see each other's face.

Stefanos began to giggle, he began to laugh. What,

said Yiorgos the Apeface, what is it? Stefanos laughed and laughed. What is it, cried Yiorgos the Apeface. This, my grandson, he said, is your inheritance. Then they rode home. Before he climbed out of the carriage Stefanos gave Yiorgos the Apeface the histories wrapped in an old cloth.

Now in the histories of Stefanos there was the story of St. Vaia which scandalised the entire village. The League of Good Men declared it a scandal. Pappous Yiorgos was angry at Stefanos the lunatic for this outrage. After all, he said, my wife was related to St. Vaia. Vaia continued to treat Theodosios with contempt. The story of St. Vaia which came from the histories of Stefanos is well known because Yiorgos the Apeface made it into a song.

In the song of Yiorgos the Apeface there was no brave Eminent Citizen to drive out the Turks. St. Vaia did not give her life to save her husband or her faith. Why, in those days, the song said, the village was a Tsifliki which belonged to Agha Emred. Agha Emred was a huge Turk who ruled the village kindly. If people's crops failed, they were exempt from paying the Agha's tax. In fact Agha Emred didn't concern himself much with the village at all. He had enough on his hands running his own household which consisted of his five industrious wives, his seven squabbling sons and his

Beloved Mustaphaki whom he had brought back from one of his many visits to Armenia.

Once he had settled the squabbles of his seven sons, had overseen his wife's work, there was nothing he liked to do more than to drink raki and to stroke the golden back of his Beloved Mustaphaki. The Beloved Mustaphaki had a beautiful golden body. He had been like this when he came from Armenia, and in the summer he would strip off and lie sunning himself on the roof. And from their windows the women and the men would watch the naked Mustaphaki. In this village the handsome lads were soft and pale. But the Beloved Mustaphaki worshipped the sun, the Mustaphaki's golden body was more wonderful than all the handsome young lads put together. Vaia saw the Mustaphaki's young body all aglow from her window. She neglected her housework and spent hours in her bedroom watching the Mustaphaki.

The song said that when Stellios the Eminent Citizen came to get his young bride, she hid in the pahni where the horses and donkeys ate from. And on their wedding night in the big white house young Vaia ran home screaming. When her parents forced her to return to her husband's house, Vaia stayed mostly in her room and watched the golden body of the Mustaphaki.

Despite the strict eye of her mother-in-law and the guarding eye of Emred, Vaia met the Mustaphaki by the river. Vaia began doing her washing by the river where only the most dedicated women went. This pleased the mother-in-law. The Mustaphaki took the Agha's camels to the river. This pleased the seven squabbling sons who complained about that lazy Mustaphaki who did nothing but lie around in the sun all day.

Vaia and the Mustaphaki lay together, behind the rock, behind the tree, behind the river. They struggled with each other deep in the sand and unearthed scorpions, which buried themselves even deeper to avoid the hot sun. When there was no one in sight the Mustaphaki would wash Vaia's body in the river, scrubbing her down with one of her mother-in-law's scarves. Then Vaia would go home soaked and say how the strong current had taken the scarf and she had dived in after it and nearly drowned.

Sometimes they fell asleep together behind the rock. And one of the Mustaphaki's camels would wander off and the Mustaphaki never bothered to find it. He just went back to Emred one camel short—told of how they had been attacked by wolves and the camel was taken. Sometimes the camel that was taken by wolves would miraculously return to Emred. But Emred enjoyed the Mustaphaki's tales so much that he would humour the Mustaphaki. For many years, Yiorgos the Apeface sings, the sun shone bright, the crops grew tall, and the wives had many children.

Then the Mustaphaki appeared on the roof one day with his beautiful buttocks savaged. After that he was not seen for weeks. Yiayia Pourthitsa, the old nurse who cleaned the Agha's house, said that the Mustaphaki was locked up in a room, tied to the Agha's bed. She said the Mustaphaki ran in circles as far as his rope would go. People did not believe the ravings of yiayia Pourthitsa, but still they were uneasy. When Emred ordered all the dogs shot, no one dared complain and the village square filled with piles and piles of dead mongrels. Meriklis the Grave-digger and Kostas the Butcher put them on a wagon and took them outside the village and buried them all there.

The Mustaphaki was bitten by a rabid dog. The Mustaphaki had rabies, but the Agha could not bare to kill his Beloved Mustaphaki. The Agha dug a huge hole in the courtyard and kept his Mustaphaki in the hole. He had his wives prepare the most delicious meals which he lowered down to the Mustaphaki himself. But his beloved Mustaphaki ate nothing. He ripped the food apart with his hands and threw it to the ground, and then he moaned. Sometimes his moans would get so loud that yiayia Pourthitsa would wake up from her sleep and pour a bucket of water over him.

The Agha raised his taxes, and because he was in such a mean mood no one dared complain, not even those who lost herds because they had no dogs to protect their animals. Stellios and the other Eminent Citizens offered the Agha gifts of corn, wine and women (mostly orphan girls) to appease him. The Agha took the corn and wine but was angry at these Greeks who thought that a girl might replace his Beloved Mustaphaki.

Outside the village Mirella helped Vaia give birth to her daughter. During the celebrations that followed, Vaia disappeared. Stellios found his wife lying on the ground, pressing herself into the dirt—behind the rock, behind the tree, behind the river. He brought her home, but months later she left again. She took Stellios' gun. She went to the hole. She shot the Beloved Mustaphaki straight through the heart.

The shot woke up the household of the Agha. When he found his beloved Mustaphaki dead, he sent two of his sons to set the village on fire. The people fled to the mountain. And Stellios the Eminent Citizen watched the great fires burning the houses down. The Agha burnt to death in his house (while he sobbed over the golden body of his Beloved Mustaphaki) with his five industrious wives and five of his squabbling sons. The other two escaped.

They pulled poor Vaia out of that fire, sings Yiorgos the Apeface, they want to know why she killed the Mustaphaki. Perhaps she told them that she loved the Mustaphaki. Perhaps she told them nothing. The song says that no matter what, Vaia had a bloody ending. Bloody enough for a sainthood.

That was the story of St. Vaia that Yiorgos the Apeface sang. When pappous Yiorgos heard about this

113

he became angry. Stella had never seen him so angry before. He threw his grandson out of the house. For weeks he went about the house muttering something about the gypsies. Vaia too was angry. She cursed Theodosios. She was certain it was her husband who had given the histories to her son. The pappous forbade her to go to the kafeneio and see her son. Vaia wanted to kill her husband. But secretly what made her really angry was to know that her son had not been cured of his reading habit, that her son must have been reading all along.

And on the next night Yiorgos the Apeface did not put the chairs and tables out. That day no one had seen him standing on the verandah pounding octopus. On the verandah lay the barrel that had once held the wild cherry drink, with an axe through it. Flies hovered above the sticky floor boards. Rumour spread that the League of Good Men had closed the kafeneio of Yiorgos the Apeface. Pourthitsa, who lived in a big house on the road leading out of the village, said that she saw a horse-drawn cart leaving the village. And on this cart was a huge wooden crate. There was something knocking inside. There was something ungodly about that crate, she said. She believed the crate was going to Paris. These are just the ravings of Pourthitsa, the villagers said.

Theodosios went to see Vaia to comfort her. Vaia was weaving at the loom when Theodosios came to see her. **114**

He tried to explain something to her by telling her a story of what had once happened between a father and a son.

There was once a man, a young man, Theodosios began, who got married and lived with his wife. One night his father sent word to him that he was ill and the son should come and spend the night with him. But it was a very cold winter's night and the man stayed home with his wife, saying he would come tomorrow.

Don't tell me, Vaia said. His father dies.

No, he lives to be over ninety. Though he never asks anything of the son again, because it is like something is broken between them. The son forgets all about that incident until he himself is an old man. Then he remembers it and . . .

And he dies, Vaia said.

No, he lives to be over ninety also. But he has a dream. That's how he remembers the incident. And in this dream his father, who by this stage has been dead for some years, stands by his son's bed and says to him, You should have come. That night when I needed you, you should have come. He has this dream every night for the rest of his life.

Well, Theodosios said, and he was choking back tears.

Well what? Vaia said.

What did you think of the story? he said.

It's just a story, she said.

But what about the man?

What about him?

He has that nightmare for thirty years.

Well he can just suck shit, she said.

Vaia continued weaving at the loom, and even began whistling (something she never did before). Theodosios put on his hat and left.

That first night people gathered outside and waited for the kafeneio to open, some began to mourn because the kafedzis was murdered. They sent messengers to the Liaris household, but got no reply. That was the first night the kafeneio did not open. That was a sad and lonely Sunday for this village.

The people of the village woke up the next day feeling nauseous and with a terrible pain behind their eyes. It only struck them on that day that at the kafeneio of Yiorgos the Apeface one could drink as much raki as one liked and never wake up with a hangover. That day no one saw the League of Good Men. That day everyone went about their work in a very sluggish, absent-minded sort of a way. That day the people of this usually productive village did hardly anything at all. The work that was done that day was mostly all wrong, so that the next two days had to be spent undoing it.

Just before sunrise Theodosios and his men returned to work the fields and the foreigners packed up their

116

tents. They rode out of the village in forty carriages. In the leading carriage sat the tribe of beautiful dark women. Many of them were pregnant and their round bellies were just beginning to show. The villagers stood on their balconies and spat at them.

In the early hours of that day Young Koulousios slit his wife's throat with a scythe.

That day the girl with the big flapping ears came to the village to see her betrothed. She sat in yiayia Stella's kitchen sobbing. She had heard, she said, that he was hairy, but in a manly, handsome sort of a way. And now they told her he was a freak. Why, the world was full of freaks, she sobbed. The yiayia had to admit that, apart from those ears, she was a pretty little thing. For her troubles Vaia gave her a bag of vegetables and money for the bus fare home.

HOW DOES YIORGOS THE APEFACE COME TO SEE AND TO LOVE AGAPE?

How does Yiorgos the Apeface come to see and to love Agape? Before we talk of love we must talk of words. In this village words had a life of their own. Why, on that very same night when Yiorgos the Apeface sang the song of St. Vaia, the League of Good Men knew of it. And on that very same night Yiorgos the Apeface knew that the League of Good Men were planning to seize him. We might say that Yiorgos the Apeface had enemies—agents, spying in the kafeneio. We might also say that Yiorgos the Apeface had friends, admirers and well-wishers. But it is perhaps truer to say that this is just the way of words in this village.

Yiorgos the Apeface closed the kafeneio early. And, having nowhere else to hide, he went to the brothel. But as it happened the League of Good Men were also due in the brothel later that very night. Now all the whores gathered around Yiorgos the Apeface as he told

118

his story. They were so full of wonder. These women had been with some ugly men, but they had never seen a man like this.

When he finished his story, Mirella took him aside so the whores could talk amongst themselves. In the end they decided to help him because they had heard he was a good cook and they knew his songs were funny.

When the League of Good Men arrived with the Schoolmaster and the Doctor they were greeted with good cheer and the best of Mirella's wine. From Mirella's room, where Yiorgos the Apeface hid, he heard them drinking and planning his murder. The League of Good Men and their two companions were in a particularly miserly mood. Someone complained about the price of the whores and the Doctor worried about disease. And neither the wine nor the meal the whores offered did anything to appease them.

They complained to Mirella that she had never offered Agape of the Glowing Face to them. Why, they said, they had heard stories of her from tobacco merchants and travelling tinkers. Was it right that the most eminent men of the village should not be offered what was given to strangers and tinkers? Mirella explained that Agape of the Glowing Face was a common girl. She spat in the square; she went to church to stare at the faces of the saints and then left halfway through the Priest's service; she ran down the street, like a silly

119

casia, when it was snowing a blizzard outside and every
sensible person was sitting by the fire. The only friend
she had was a pig. (Agape befriended the only wild
boar she came across on her hunting trips with Meta.
Every evening it came running through the streets and
wandered into the courtyard where Agape fed it chunks
of watermelon and washed its snout with water poured
from a porcelain vase. Everyone knew this was Agape's
boar and no one in the village dared touch it.) As for
her glowing face, it was in all truth a terrible glow, a
dangerous thing.

But the League of Good Men said they would not be
outdone by drunken tinkers. One at a time Mirella led
them to Agape. (The Doctor, who often came to the
brothel but never slept with the whores because he was
afraid of disease, stayed in the courtyard and got very
drunk.)

Now it is time to tell you how Yiorgos the Apeface
came to see and to love Agape of the Glowing Face.
Mirella's room was a room placed in the middle of the
house with a number of peepholes so that from her
room you could see into almost every room of the
brothel. Mirella took Yiorgos the Apeface to these holes
so he could see what would happen to his enemies.
Being a dignified man, Yiorgos the Apeface declined
Mirella's offer. But the cries of men awakened his curiosity and at last he came to watch. This is what Yiorgos
the Apeface saw.

120

Yiorgos saw each of the men enter Agape's room. As they were fucking her he saw her glowing face burst into that sudden flash of light. (Something like the light that shines in the eyes of a fox on a summer's night when it stares up at chickens sitting in trees, long enough to make them fall out. But not exactly like this. Something like the light that reflects off the white-wash on a hot Mediterranean afternoon. But not exactly like this either.) A light so piercing that even from the distance where he stood Yiorgos shielded his eyes. And when they had finished fucking, after they had looked directly into her glowing face, the men bolted upright, looked about the room, eyes blinking in confusion before they lay their heads down next to hers and died. Their faces were calm but their fists were clenched and their bodies curled inwards as if they were guarding some precious knowledge. They died so swiftly, so surely that their state could never be confused with sleep. That is the terrible pleasure that Yiorgos the Apeface came to desire.

At the end of that night Meta loaded the whole lot of them in a crate and took them to an empty field on the marshland where the fires of the foreigners were still burning. She believed it proper for people to be buried on their land. And the whores all agreed that even miserly men deserved a proper burial. The Doctor, seeing all his companions had left, put on his hat and

121

staggered home too. That is how the fateful night ended.

But there are two things still left unsaid. The first thing you must know is that Agape of the Glowing Face was not a murderer. She was much too peaceful to kill anyone; she did not know that her face could kill. But even if she had known, she would still have been innocent. She is one of those people who are born innocent and stay that way. That is the beauty of Agape of the Glowing Face. Yiorgos the Apeface saw this. The second thing is that despite all those rumours about the mystery of his manhood (some said that in its potent state it was so large it could split a woman in two) Yiorgos the Apeface was thirty-two years of age and he had not yet known a woman.

THAT WEEK YIORGOS THE APEFACE WROTE
SEVEN LETTERS

That week Yiorgos the Apeface wrote seven letters. He stayed in the brothel for seven days and on each day he wrote a letter to Agape of the Glowing Face. And when the letters were finished, he went to see his father. He asked Theodosios to deliver these letters, one a week, to Agape of the Glowing Face. Theodosios was shocked to see his son but he took the letters and promised to take them to the brothel. From there Yiorgos the Apeface made his way to the kafeneio, whistling cheerfully.

Theodosios put on his coat and his best hat and went to tell Vaia that their son was still alive. Yiayia Stella was not at all surprised by this news; she had seen the bones glowing. When Vaia and Theodosios were alone, he showed her their son's letters and she asked what they said. These are letters of love, Theodosios said. Then he went home.

But that afternoon Vaia followed Theodosios to his

house. She asked him to read the letters to her. Theodosios put on his father's glasses, he picked up a letter. He concentrated so hard all the veins on his head began to throb. Then he put the letter down and admitted that he could not read. Vaia became very sad, and Theodosios touched her on the back of the neck. Theodosios declared that he would learn to read. He said he was from a family of educated men and reading was in his blood. Before Vaia went home she shared a meal with her husband.

Now, that Sunday people noticed that the sign of the wild cherry drink was back in the window again. People saw Yiorgos the Apeface himself pounding octopus till it was tender on the verandah. As Yiorgos the Apeface wiped the tables and chairs down, people gathered outside the kafeneio and waited for it to open. And when the door opened, the people rushed in and they cheered for Yiorgos the Apeface, the best kafedzis the village had ever known. The people piled in to the kafeneio. They drank and ate and laughed like usual. But the truth was that there was something very different about the kafeneio that Sunday. What it was exactly is hard to say. But everyone felt that something had changed.

On that night something quite different happened. Yiorgos the Apeface sang that night. That night his songs were not about people. At least not any person in particular. No one there could really tell you what

124

they were about. In the songs of Yiorgos the Apeface there was something sad, something unbearable. Some people cried, others blushed, others were confused. There was a little bit here about the sound of running water, a little bit there about a shady tree. It seemed to make no sense, no sense at all. But the warm gentle waves of the voice of Yiorgos the Apeface went on and on. And it was as if these warm waves of sound moved through the room of the kafeneio, slowly caressing the bodies of all the people who were listening, for they were overcome with a terrible desire. As soon as the songs were over, people rushed out of the kafeneio to go home, to tear off their clothes and fall upon each other. And behind a tree, just outside the kafeneio, the Priest of Casia lay underneath the heavy thighs of his cook.

Theodosios woke up the next morning and began painting his house. He could not remember Vaia's face. And for a week he saw auras, had a buzzing in his left ear and little sparkles in his vision. He painted the walls and ceilings of his room with huge yellow flowers, like a field of giant chamomile. Then he became afraid that his wife may recognise the allusion to the brothel. To make it less obvious he also painted the kitchen with blossoming almond trees. His father's room, which was the shed outside the house, he painted with a field of fig trees. A field where there was no one to pick the figs and they lay on the ground open, glistening in the sun.

125

The outside of the house he painted with a field of strong and sombre tobacco plants.

Every night Vaia went to cook a meal for her husband. Theodosios spent all day working in the fields and spent all night learning to read. Vaia would tell yiayia Stella she was going to visit an old theia but she would go by the back way to her husband's. She swore her husband to secrecy about the visits. Apart from Stefanos (for whom they always kept a plate of beans), no one else should have known about these visits. But by that very same night every man, woman and child of the village knew that Vaia was seeing her husband. For the gossips this was even better than Old Koulousios and his daughter-in-law. There was talk for a while that Vaia was pregnant again. People whispered about all sorts of monsters she might give birth to. They said someone should tell Vaia about the place where Fatime went for her countless abortions. But yiayia Stella went to church every day and lit a candle of joy.

The seven letters were kept in a box with other precious things. Theodosios persevered with his reading. Every Sunday Vaia would ask him how he was going. And he would reply that it was not easy learning to read and that she must be patient. Then he would open the box and, taking a letter out, would read an occasional word. And Vaia would clasp her hands together in delight. Finally, one Saturday, Theodosios

126

sent a young boy to tell Vaia that she should come early that Sunday. Vaia realised what this meant.

She was nearly sixty. She took off all her clothes and looked at her body for the first time since those long baths with her son. She was not unhappy with what she saw. It was just that this was a different body. It was as though one day, without her knowing it, someone had taken her young body and given her this one in its place. She did not think it an unfair exchange. She prepared herself with all the anxiety of a young bride.

Theodosios and Vaia never finished their meal. Theodosios lit the lamp and Vaia took out the letters with trembling fingers. Theodosios had learnt to read from his father's books. He had promised Vaia that he would not read the letters without her. Theodosios took out his father's glasses and put them on. He cleared his throat and at last he began to read.

Vaia heard the words but did not understand the letter. There was something about a shady tree which gave relief from the hot sun and a little bit about the sound of running water. Vaia asked Theodosios if he was perhaps reading it wrong. Theodosios was angry with the impatience of his wife. To prove his skills he took out a thick book that belonged to Stefanos and began to read from that. Vaia urged him to go on with the letters. But each one was the same.

Vaia slipped out in the early hours of that morning without a word to her husband. Theodosios continued reading the letters to himself over and over again. When he had finished, he felt sad, and he decided to deliver the letters to the whore as he had promised.

But just behind the brothel the two elder Koulousiathes brothers tried to strangle Theodosios, because they said, they were in mourning for the wife of young Koulousios and objected to the colours of Theodosios' house. People asked, if they were really in mourning, then what were they doing hanging about the brothel? Meta came upon the two brothers whilst they were beating Theodosios, she picked them up by the scruff of their necks and pushed them to the ground. She held both of them down and spat in their eyes. After being rescued by Meta, Theodosios felt too ashamed to walk into the brothel, and so he returned home with the letters.

The next Sunday, Vaia came again. Theodosios had not expected her to come. She was dressed in black, wore uncombed hair and had dirt under her nails. Theodosios read the second letter to her, and she was embarrassed by it. She called it nonsense. But this time it did not matter because she had been expecting nothing. Every week Vaia continued to eat with her husband and to hear him read a letter.

What nonsense that son of mine writes, Vaia would say.

Then they'd put the letters down and drink Turkish   **128** coffee, so much that each of them lay awake till dawn. On warm nights they sat outside and Theodosios would read with a small lamp. He became a good reader. He practised every day. He was so good that Vaia came to love the sound of the words rolling off his tongue. They talked about their marriage. Sometimes they stopped because of the sound of crickets and croaking frogs. Sometimes they lit a fire and roasted corn, sometimes they touched. There was something that she was going to tell her husband. She was going to say that yiayia Stella had grown old. Vaia had only just seen it and she had come to understand the son's nightmare. That is what she was going to say to him. Vaia waited eagerly to read the next letter.

One day yiayia Stella came to the brothel to visit Mirella, as she had promised to. And Mirella saw then just how close Stella had come to death. When yiayia Stella gave the bones to Vaia, she was preparing herself to die. The bones were not a gift from mother to daughter. The bones were useless. They could not quench the daughter's old sadness, and in fact they were not meant to. In the Days of Progress, yiayia Stella decided that she was dying, and all of herself that she had given to the world (and, God knows, she had given a lot) she took back. When she took back what she had given to her husband, to the village and to her daughter, it was like she had drained the colours and the waters out of everything. And everything around her became grey and dry. Dying is grey and dry.

And for days, many days, Stella did nothing but stand at the gate and watch the road. She watched people come to the village and people leave the village. She watched the road when there was no one on it. She stood by the gate, watching that road until it was so dark you could not see your own hand.

Pappous Yiorgos couldn't bear to have his wife standing by the gate watching the road any longer, so he sent Vaia to ask her mother what she was watching for. Yiayia Stella answered Vaia in words the daughter did not understand. Vaia became afraid and hurried to her father to repeat these strange words. Pappous Yiorgos repeated the words to himself over and over again so that he would never forget them. And because he loved his wife, he went to see the Schoolmaster to find out what these words might mean. The Schoolmaster said that the words must be of an ancient dialect that only the great scholars of the big towns can understand.

Pappous Yiorgos went to the town of the great scholars. For a week he paid the scholars and they consulted in their books which had words from every language. In the end, when nearly all his money had run out, the scholars told pappous Yiorgos that his wife was mad. They told him that he must return home, he must not leave his mad wife alone for another minute. With the last of his money pappous Yiorgos bought thread from a gypsy women. Beautiful coloured thread for a mad wife. Silk thread in colours he had never seen before. He spent all his money on the thread so that on his last night in the town he had to sleep out in the street.

Pappous Yiorgos returned home with nothing. And as he was walking into the village he saw her bent figure and her little face pushed up against the gate, watching the road that led into the village. His heart ached. That's when he knew the meaning of the words she had said. She had said that all men are from one town and sooner or later they return to that town. His heart ached because there was nothing he could do for her.

One day yiayia Stella lost interest in the road altogether. She came inside, found the coloured threads and began weaving a beautiful tapestry, as if nothing had happened. Yiayia Stella took the bones back, she changed her mind. In the Days of Progress she could not change into a bear. And, of course, once you have known death you cannot unknow it. The weariness remains (Stella grew wrinkled and bent, old overnight). But she gave herself back to the world, and the waters broke and colour ran through everything. Remember, such a change of mind is in many ways more mysterious even than changing into a bear.

131   The harvest was remarkable. The village filled with colour. Tomato plants, especially, keeled over from the weight of their tremendous fruit. The wines that summer were delicious, the oils were thick and pure. It seemed that everyone's donkey was pregnant that summer. Everyone's donkey was having twins, and even triplets were not unheard of. People sold these donkeys in the donkey markets of neighbouring towns and villages. The donkey trade was an unexpected and prosperous one that summer.

All the time pappous Yiorgos grumbled and nagged his wife for being so stupid. She had made him buy a mule instead of a donkey last year. If they had a donkey, he said, they would have had something to sell. We don't need to sell anything, you greedy old man, yiayia Stella said.

But that summer their mule defied the curse of the Virgin Mary. They say when the good Virgin was searching for a place to give birth, the first stable she opened was filled with mules. One mule kicked her in the belly, and she cursed all mules. So that is why today you have female mules and male mules, but mules never bear young.

That summer one of their mules gave birth to a mule. They told no one about it. They fed the baby mule from a big bottle, and they raised it themselves. Yiayia Stella and pappous Yiorgos stayed awake at night and spoke to each other in hushed whispers about the mystery of

132

their house. The house where a mule gave birth to a mule.

There were many odd marriages that summer. The Priest of Casia married his cook Pourthitsa. But the biggest surprise was the marriage of the son of the Maranathes. When he was only fifteen he had brought his sweetheart home six months pregnant. She was a black girl of gypsy stock. His mother chased her out of the house. His mother said she was a whore. The son didn't know what to do and the girl left the village. Now four years later the son went to the city and he found her on a street with her daughter, selling boxes of tissues and plastic combs.

The week that Theodosios announced the sharing of the fields it had been forty degrees every day. At his son's kafeneio Theodosios announced that the fields of the League of Good Men, the fields of the marshland, would be shared amongst the people of the village. Every single family would get something (even the Turks and the whores) and those with little or no land would get two fields. People did not know whether Theodosios was a criminal, a mad man or a saint. He gave to widows, to Turks, he gave to the beggars and to the rich. Some were confused, others were furious. Could Theodosios do this, they wanted to know? The widows of the League of Good Men had been celebrating at the kafeneio every week since the disappearance of their husbands, and they made no claims to the fields. The Doctor might have complained, but he too had been at the kafeneio drinking wild cherry drink along with raki and chewing on dried chillies. So the village celebrated for a whole week.

There was so much food that people just ate and ate. They fed their pigs and chickens on roast meat. In the end they buried food in their back yards. There were fireworks every night. With that long heat, yiayia Stella said it was a miracle the village never went up in flames.

EVERY DAY YIORGOS THE APEFACE STOOD OUTSIDE, WAITING FOR A REPLY TO HIS LETTERS

Every day Yiorgos the Apeface stood outside, waiting for a reply to his letters. When the sun went down, the arrogant boar trotted past him, through the gate that was left open for it, and sat in the courtyard waiting for her too. Every day Agape came out with her glowing face, her porcelain vase and half a watermelon under her arm. She fed the wild boar and then went back inside without even casting Yiorgos a glance. So every night Yiorgos the Apeface returned to his kafeneio and sang those sad songs. The kafeneio of Yiorgos the Apeface was a popular place, and as each day passed his songs became sadder and the desire of the crowd more urgent.

There was abundance and prosperity in the village. Yiayia Stella lit a candle of joy to the icon of St. Vaia. Then one day she found the icon of St. Vaia smeared with shit. As this was a very bad omen, she thought it best not to tell anyone. But because of the way of words in the village, by that very same night every man, woman and child was asking: Who was it that smeared the icon of St. Vaia with shit? Someone said the Priest of Casia did not want people to come to his church. They said the Priest of Casia would rather lie in bed all day entwined with his cook. Someone said that the angry souls of the League of Good Men did this. Someone replied that souls such as those of the League of Good Men would certainly be in heaven. The Doctor asked: Was there shit in heaven?

At night Yiorgos the Apeface may have been the revered kafedzis who sang those unearthly songs. But by day he was this ugly man who spent all day peering into the brothel but never went inside. He got burnt by the sun, poked fun at by the whores, punched by the men who used the whores, and shat on by the birds that flew over him. Because he was her grandson, Meta brought him a glass of water and a piece of cheese. She never asked him what he was doing there. Slowly the days grew shorter and the nights longer. The first rains fell, but still Yiorgos the Apeface stood outside the brothel waiting for Agape to reply to his letters.

Pappous Yiorgos thought it was disgraceful that a grandson of his was standing outside a brothel. So he went to see him to persuade him to come home. That's when he told his grandson about poor old Pawonia.

Nestor and Yiorgos had this older sister who they

didn't talk about much because she had brought great disgrace upon them. Her problem was that she could never warm to any man. Pawonia, the villagers called her. Her parents could not understand it. They always thought that she would make a wonderful wife. She was not a bad-looking girl. She was a good cook, hardworking in the fields and very respectable. No scandal was connected with her name, until after she married that is. (Of course she married, if you could call that a marriage; it lasted barely a year.) Pawonia's husband hung himself off the branches of an old walnut tree. There seemed to be no reason for this. People said it was his wife that drove him to it. She cannot love anyone. This woman has no womb they said, she ruins everything. See how she did not cry at his funeral. Pawonia had never cried they said, never shed a tear in her life.

But this wasn't true. The pappous remembered that once her bleeding days had begun she became afraid of the dark. She kept everyone up, especially in the winter when the night comes so early. As soon as the lamps were turned out Pawonia would begin to weep. Yiayia Eugeneia would take the young girl to her bed and comfort her. Yiayia Eugeneia had nursed Pawonia as a child and she could not bear to hear her cry. But yiayia Eugeneia did not last long. One day when she was picking walnuts she fell out of the tree and broke her guts. (This family had no luck with walnut trees.) At the funeral Pawonia did not cry. She held her two younger brothers by the hand and when Nestor and Yiorgos cried she smacked them on the bum, telling them to shut up. There is a sadness, she said, that is beyond tears.

They were wrong, too, about Pawonia not being able to love. Love came to Pawonia. But it came too late and people are not always kind. It began one summer. Her family worked in a field next to his. At lunch the two families shared their blankets and ate onions and sardines together. Now these parts are known for their fierce electric storms. And if you are caught in the field during one of these storms there is no place to run, no place to hide except under a blanket. It was under his blanket that Pawonia hid when the rains came and the thunder rumbled. He was the thirteen-year-old son of a cousin of hers.

Of course the sensible people agreed that life was miserable and love, no matter when it came or what form it took, should not be wasted. As for Pawonia, she lost her sense altogether. She wore cherries behind her ear and asked people in the kafeneio what she should do to make the young boy love her. Some people wanted to have a good laugh at her expense. That's the way people are. They told her the young lad would certainly love her if she spent a night outside his house.

It was a freezing winter's night. She put on her warmest dress and steeled herself against the cold.

138

Inside the young lad was sleeping and his parents could hear their crazy cousin Pawonia calling out to the wind. Blow cold wind, she cried, blow, for tonight I spend with you and tomorrow night with my husband. But by morning the whole village heard that Pawonia had frozen to death.

Here Yiorgos the Apeface interrupted his pappou. Did the young lad know then just how much Pawonia had loved him, he asked.

The pappous seemed surprised at this question. That, he said, is not important.

Then what is the point of your story, pappou?

The pappous thought about this for a while. The point of my story? The point is that winter is just not a good season for lovers. With this the pappous returned home.

But Yiorgos the Apeface continued to wait for a reply to the letters while Theodosios and Vaia continued to share them. They read them together again and again. They were not malicious parents. Why, Vaia had sacrificed her whole life for her son, and in his own way Theodosios had tried too. It was just that they forgot to whom the letters belonged. And it seemed to them that these letters were theirs, that they had always belonged to them. At that time they could not have imagined it otherwise.

In fact, while they shared the letters, they spoke **139** mostly of their son. Vaia told Theodosios how much she loved their son. She told him that love kept her awake at night. Then Theodosios admitted something to Vaia. He told her that he had always been afraid of becoming a father. He told her it had always terrified him. He told her that having a child, a son, especially a son, was like having a monster that took everything from you.

One day that terrible thing, the one yiayia Stella had been waiting for ever since she found the icons smeared with shit, happened. The field of fig trees—the field where there was no one to pick the figs and so they lay open on the ground glistening in the sun—went up in smoke. It was after all only painted on a wall. (The whole shed burnt down one night, and no one heard Stefanos cry out.) But who was it that lit the fire? Was it the Koulousiathes brothers exacting their revenge on the colourful house of Theodosios? Was it Meta who wore a red dress to her husband's funeral, danced on his grave and stole the food that was left out for his soul? Or did the lamp fall on Stefanos' books while he slept?

By far the biggest celebration of all was the funeral of Stefanos who died in the fire. On the day of the funeral a wreath of flowers hung on the door of every house. And the coffin was made of a beautiful dark wood that the people of that village had never seen before. On top of it was a cross of solid gold. People said that Theodosios must have sold his soul for this funeral. Eight men were needed to hold the coffin.   **140**

Behind it came Theodosios, his brothers and sisters, Vaia and her family. Fifty-six professional mourners were hired, and their wails could be heard all the way to the town of Zandelli. Behind followed the entire village, including the Turks. Then there was a choir of twenty-one young men. And right at the end there were twenty-one young virgins, each with a basket of white rose-buds. They filled the street with flowers. After the golden coffin was placed in the grave, all the brothers and sisters threw a handful of dirt in to it. When Meta walked past, she spat in it. When it was Theodosios' turn he threw his whole body into the grave and wailed. The choir chanted. When Theodosios would not climb out of the grave, the pappous climbed in and with the help of Kostas the Butcher pulled him out.

Instead of a plate of wheat and a glass of water being left in the courtyard for the soul, there were loaves of bread, borek, pots of egg-lemon chicken soup, salted meats and little casks of wine. Instead of three days, this food was out there for three weeks. Stefanos' spirit must have been very hungry, people said, because the food disappeared every night. But others knew that it was Meta (she hated to see food wasted) who came in the night, and that the whores feasted on the food meant for Stefanos' soul.

After the funeral, strange little clouds appeared over the mountain and it snowed, the first snow of the year. The children ran out in their good clothes and screamed in the snow. They screamed when the cold wind blew. Their faces grew rosy and their noses froze. On that day Yiorgos the Apeface knew winter had come early that year and that Agape would never answer his letters. So he gave up waiting. He returned to his kafeneio and he took the sign of the wild cherry drink out of the window.

In those days the ghost of St. Vaia appeared in the village. She would visit the Turks and beat them up. She would tell them that St. Vaia wants them to leave the fields of the marshland, to leave the village altogether. She would beat them up in ways which left terrible bruises. Some Turks took their families and left. Then it was discovered that young Greek boys were painting their faces with rice powder and dressing in long white robes. One St. Vaia was captured by the Turks and had her balls cut off. And after this the visitations of St. Vaia stopped.

Yiorgos the Apeface barred himself inside the kafeneio. The kafeneio had not opened for weeks. Every Sunday night, despite the cold, people came and stood outside the kafeneio, hoping it might open. But it never did. Even though everyone had plenty of food, people still grumbled. They said the family would pay for disturbing the order of nature like this. It was a terrible business, terrible indeed when you did not know where you stood with anyone any more. That is what these people said. With the giving away of the fields, one could not see who was rich and who was poor. Why the Turks, they had got so proud, you might think that they were Greeks. Then there was Meta, neither man nor woman, and her grandson both man and animal. How was one to know anything in a world like this?

On Sundays people hung about the kafeneio. They lit fires and roasted whistling snails and chestnuts. Children aimed their stones at Yiorgos the Apeface who came out in the evenings and stood at the window watching. Whenever a window was smashed the parents cheered. Whore-lover, they cried out, coward, half-man. They spat on the ground and shook their fists up at the hairy kafedzis, but secretly they hoped that if they waited there long enough he might open the kafeneio.

As for Yiorgos the Apeface, it was not the crowd that he came to the window to watch. Every evening Agape's boar ran through the square on its way to the brothel. Yiorgos the Apeface stood by the window hoping to catch a glimpse of the pig. He became fascinated by the fierce beauty of Agape's boar.

A rumour spread through the village that Yiorgos the Apeface was going to fight the boar. A fight to the death for Agape's love. Mirella, they said, was cutting off the buttocks of the whores to feed the pig. Agape of the Glowing Face mixed a special feed of watermelon, rolled oats and flesh. Men who used the brothel confirmed that many of the whores there had only half a bum. But the men who used the whores were mostly drunks and generally men whose word could not be trusted.

When Vaia heard the rumour she remembered then that the letters belonged to her son. She ran to her husband's house only to find the windows painted black and the doors barred shut. When he would not open the front door, she began to beat it down with her body. She yelled at him that the letters did not belong to them any longer. She yelled at Theodosios that he must take them to the whore. But Theodosios was in mourning for his father and he would not come out. Vaia kept throwing her body against the door till she broke her arm and pappous Yiorgos came to bring her home. Why, the pappous thought, everyone had gone mad. (In this story that is the last time Vaia speaks to Theodosios. In fact Vaia never thinks of Theodosios again. Vaia found a wheat sack, dyed it black, cut out holes for the arms, the head, and put it on. She also found the veil she had worn as a lyhouna and covered her face with that.)

Yiorgos the Apeface heard the puzzling rumour from Pourthitsa the Matchmaker when he came to the square to collect his food from her. Instead of spitting at him like the crowd usually did, they stared at him in awed silence. He asked Pourthitsa what this silence meant. That's when she told him about the rumours. At first he thought it was just the ravings of Pourthitsa. He wondered who could have begun such a rumour. But the more he thought about it the more sense the fight seemed to make. And though he knew that he had never spoken a word of such a fight to anyone, he wondered if he had not somehow begun this rumour himself. He wondered if perhaps words are not written in us long before they are ever spoken. This is the last thought he had before the pig came running across his path.

When he rushed at the boar, men and women alike held their breath at the sight of him. The old people thought of Meta as a young mother. They were reminded of her powerful limbs. They thought of the way she wrestled wolves and wild boars. Others thought of Nestor and those wonderful fights on warm summer evenings with the fathers and the brothers of the ruined girls. But Yiorgos the Apeface was only a kafedzis. He did not have the strength of Meta nor the speed of Nestor. In the very first round, the boar pierced him with its huge tusks, lay him on the ground and savaged him.

When they saw that the hairy kafedzis was dead, the crowd turned on Agape's boar killing it with heavy stones. Afterwards they collected the boar so they could roast it and then they filed past looking at the body of Yiorgos the Apeface. It was Pourthitsa who began to wail when she looked at his face. Though his body was mauled his face was unharmed except for a bloody cut

145

that ran from his temple down to his chin. He wasn't much of a fighter, but my God his blood was sweet. Sweeter than Nestor's had ever been, whispered the old women. A panic gripped the crowd and so they dropped Agape's boar and fled.

The news spread, and people locked themselves inside their houses. Vaia and Agape went to the square to collect their dead. Agape roasted the boar and brought it to the brothel for the whores to eat. (Agape had inherited Meta's hate of waste.) Vaia carried her son out to what had been Meta's fields and buried him under the olive tree.

Eventually people went about their business again, as people always do. Kostas the Butcher took over the kafeneio, but it was never the same. Without the songs, the kafeneio of Yiorgos the Apeface became a sad and lonely sort of place. People did not talk about him. People forgot about him, people were not interested in talking about anything any more. When this happened, Kostas the Butcher bought himself a new mince machine and closed down the kafeneio.

For many years the crops were good and people worked hard in their fields. But eventually the marsh reclaimed its land. The fields of the marshland became so soggy that the crops would rot. The young people went to the city to find work. One by one the whores left. Theodosios also left the village. Before he left he sent Vaia a package which she threw in the fire without

146

smelling it or licking it. It was on a dark winter's night that Theodosios stole out. The first anyone knew of it was when the Jewish money-lenders came to collect the money he had borrowed for his father's funeral. Pappous Yiorgos paid the debt because he said it was undignified for a son-in-law of his to be in debt.

NOW ONE EVENING, AFTER MANY EVENINGS, THE WEARY AND INSIGNIFICANT MAN WALKED INTO THE VILLAGE *Now one evening, after many evenings, the weary and insignificant man walked into the village. He sat down in the square and sang a song. No one bothered about him. No one stopped to listen. (Vaia walked right past him on the way to the spring amidst the rocks where she went every day. Vaia was still hiding in her black sack.) When the man finished his song, he packed up his things and left. From that day, this man came to sing every evening. And no one ever bothered to listen to him. Where he came from no one knew, and no one cared. He became part of the village, like the large stone on the cobbled street where he sat.*

But at about this time Agape of the Glowing Face began to carve wooden figures of men with beast's heads. She would go out to the courtyard with a lamp, a piece of wood and her knife. She waited for the sun to go down and then began her ghastly carvings. One day I asked her (expecting no reply,

148

*Agape had not spoken to anyone since the death of her boar)
what these figures meant. That day she spoke to us.*

Can't you hear him Mirella, she said.

*Meta and I listened carefully, but we could hear nothing.
That song, she said, is terribly sad. And if she were talking
about the weary and insignificant man, we told her our house
was much too far from the square for her to possibly hear
him. She said nothing after that. She just continued listening.
All we heard was the frogs croaking.*

*And now each day that passes seems exactly like the other.
For the people here, all time is like one day. All day and every
day is spent reclaiming a piece of land from the marsh. It's
an impossible task. Where the water comes from is a mystery
to me; the valley dried up years ago. Today Meta said that
someone found a fish on their field. Was it really a fish or
was it a rumour?*

SO THAT WAS THE STORY OF THIS
VILLAGE
So that was the story of this village. If you found my story somewhat puzzling all I can say is that every house has a story. For those who hear that story there is no relief, not under the shade of a tree or even behind a rock. They hear it in the voice of a stranger, in the sound of running water, they hear it everywhere. Those who hear that story must repeat it—in a tapestry woven with coloured thread, in scandalous histories, in unanswered letters, even in the ghastly carvings of Agape. Every house continues to repeat its story in any way it knows how. This is the story of my House, and I have told it to you in the only way I knew how.